GOLD FEVER

GOLD FEVER

ROBERT ANDERSON

A Black Horse Western

ROBERT HALE • LONDON

© Robert Anderson 1997
First published in Great Britain 1997

ISBN 0 7090 6062 9

Robert Hale Limited
Clerkenwell House
Clerkenwell Green
London EC1R 0HT

Photoset in North Wales by
Derek Doyle & Associates, Mold, Clwyd
Printed and bound in Great Britain by
WBC Book Manufacturers Limited,
Bridgend, Mid-Glamorgan

I

SUDDEN DEATH

'I'll see your five, and raise you ten.' The harsh voice belonged to a new face in town, but no stranger to the tables; the cards had run his way all night.

Jim Delaney stirred in his seat, and, sloughing off his more usual air of idle detachment, stared thoughtfully across the table, probing the hatchet-faced newcomer's intentions with hard-eyed resolution. The stranger met his gaze without flinching, though his lean form, dressed in neat, dark suiting, shifted restlessly under such close scrutiny. There was an elusive trace of the furtive in the man's manner that irked the gambler, despite his studied air of affability.

'Lady Luck seems to be smiling your way tonight,' he observed nonchalantly, keeping his eyes fixed on the stranger's face.

'You can say that again.' The drummer on Jim's

left, a stout man of florid countenance, broke in querulously. 'I ain't hardly held a winning hand all night.'

'My luck's been in,' admitted the stranger. His voice held a queer, high pitched nasal twang that jarred on Jim's nerves, 'but allow me credit for some skill as well.'

The overly-young cowboy making up a fourth at the little table showed his impatience at the delay by grunting audibly. 'Quit talking, and let's get on with it,' he requested shortly.

That youth had been by far the biggest loser in the game thus far, and Jim contemplated him uneasily. He'd displayed all the signs of impatience with his losses over the past few hands, but an air of suppressed excitement now hung about him, the tell-tale indication that he held good cards for once. The gambler folded at once, and nodded easily to the drummer.

'I'm out,' he confirmed.

'Me, too.' The salesman wiped a mottled kerchief across his brow, and flung his cards wearily face down on the table.

'How about you, sonny?' Hatchet-face leered nastily in the cowboy's direction, presenting the youngster with an ugly close-up of his stained and rotting teeth.

'Beat this, if you can.' The youngster, ignoring the other's provocation, carefully pushed across the last of his roll, and displayed his cards with a flourish.

'Too bad, kid,' the stranger smirked. 'Guess it's

like they say, my lucky day.' He laid down his own hand, and began to gather up the coins piled on the table.

'Just one minute, fella.' The cowboy stood up to face his tormentor. His right hand rested on the broad leather belt, a scant few inches above the battered pistol that rode on his hip. 'No one owns luck that good; you're a damned cheat.'

'Be careful what you say, sonny.' The stranger issued his warning in harshly sibilant tones. 'You might offend someone.'

'I call the facts as I see them,' the youngster returned candidly. 'You're a stinking cheat, and a liar besides.' His hand dropped to his holster and grasped the butt of the pistol nestling there, foolishly pausing to administer one last insult. 'The town will thank me for ridding it of trash like you.'

The stranger's speedy draw was a blur of motion that took the young greenhorn by surprise, and left him scrambling to clear leather in a lather of desperation. A sharp report echoed harshly around the room, bringing a sudden end to the hubbub about them, while the hatchet-faced man sagged in his seat, staring in wide-eyed surprise at the smoking pistol in Jim's grasp. A moment later the gun in his own hand exploded harmlessly into the floor, and he expired, blood still oozing slowly from the neat hole drilled over his heart.

The cowboy turned numbly to his rescuer, his own weapon barely clear of its holster. 'Gee thanks, fella,' he mumbled in staggered awe, and sat down abruptly, the blood draining from his face in pallid reaction. 'Guess I owe you one.'

'Reckon so.' Jim stood up to confront the owner of the saloon, who'd swiftly arrived upon the scene, backed up by two of his bullies carrying shotguns.

'No call for further violence,' he warned them quietly. 'This here man's no more than a cheat who tried to murder the boy.' He put away his gun, and leaned forward to pluck a pair of cards from the dead man's sleeve. 'Good at his work, too. I guessed he was cutting a ruse early on in the game, but I never once caught a whiff of him making the swap.' He threw the cards on the table and stared at the men, as if daring them to take the matter further.

'So.' The bar owner studied the gambler a moment longer, then waved back his bullies. 'I guess he got his just deserts, but I won't have any more gunplay in here, the city council don't like it.'

'No more,' agreed Jim easily. He waved the man's hands away from the money lying on the table. 'Those coins belong with my young friend, I believe.'

The other examined Jim's fixed expression and capitulated. 'Come on, lads. Let's get this mess cleared up.'

The other occupants of the saloon began to return to their business, discussing the killing in excited tones. It had happened too quickly for most of them to see, but the action had mightily impressed one incongruous figure. Tall and gaunt, he was dressed from head to foot in pale buckskins decorated with elaborate fringes, and sported a racoon- tailed beaver over his long, white-streaked hair.

'You know that man?' he demanded of one of the barmen.

'Yes, sir. Most everyone does. That there's Diamond Jim Delaney.'

'A gambler?' His eyes turned in Jim Delaney's direction, taking in the trim black suit, immaculate over a white, ruffled shirt and neat, bow-string tie.

'That's right, mister. Gunman too. Used to be a US marshal way out on the frontier, or so I heard tell.'

'If that diamond at his throat's real, he's mighty rich for a lawman.'

'Sure it's real,' the barman replied. 'That's why they call him Diamond Jim. And he's rich enough, I reckon. Earns his money gambling big-time on the river queens, but he's been right here in town over the winter months; staying at the best hotel, and keeping his hand in at the tables here.'

'He wouldn't be interested in a job, then?' The buckskin-clad man's lined face turned away from the scene even as he spoke the words, more to himself than the barman.

'No, not him,' snorted his informant confidently. 'Not if it's offered by the likes of you.'

Jim Delaney drifted slowly across to the bar and ordered whiskey, waving away the renewed appreciation of the young cow puncher. Huddled over the gloomy table, he'd appeared a smaller, older man, with deep sunken eyes, but standing by the bar with the light striking his face, he presented a different picture. His tall, rangy figure, and loose, long-limbed walk bespoke of his past, riding the wide range and keeping the law in violent frontier towns, while his face, lined by sun and sorrow, rather than age, showed a dignity at odds with his brooding expression. But his eyes attracted the most attention; piercing blue orbs, imbued with an assured stare that had more than once proved capable of disconcerting the most hardened wrong-doer.

A soft form materialized by his elbow, pressing close against his arm while she pushed forward. He stared down into a pair of bright, excited eyes, instantly recognising the girl who'd stationed herself close behind him at the game.

'I thought you'd never get to notice me,' she purred contentedly, leaning provocatively into his length.

'Sure you didn't.' The gambler's voice was weary, and the polite half-smile he pasted on his lips failed to reach so far as the cold fastnesses of his eyes.

'Aren't you going to buy me a drink?' Her face assumed a wheedling expression and Jim did as she bid, though there was no softening evident in his grim visage.

'Leave him alone, Lil.' A feminine voice dismissed the girl, who pouted, but prudently did as she was told.

'Maggie.' The gambler acknowledged her presence. 'You want a drink, too?'

'No, I don't.' The woman was older, her face starting to crumble under the ravages of time, though her figure still appeared trim and shapely, even when measured against the younger girls. 'And neither do you.'

'You've left it too late to become a mother hen, Maggie.' Then added cruelly, 'And joined the wrong profession.'

The woman wilted under his sarcastic wit, uncomfortably aware he'd hit on a soft spot.

'That's not like you, Jim.'

'And what is like me?' Jim's face maintained its stony expression. He knew he'd hurt the woman, but remained too engrossed in his own afflictions to care over-much. So what if she was upset? They'd sat and talked a few times; she'd been a friendly face, but no more than that. He didn't want anyone around who would deflect his thoughts from his own shortcomings.

'You're upset, Jim.' The madame reached out a comforting hand, but her face blanched when he turned on her viciously.

'Damned right I'm upset. I just killed a man.' Jim's voice rang ugly, dangerous, and a manic gleam sparked in his eyes.

'A cheat and a thief, one who would have killed that boy if you hadn't interfered,' she reminded him. 'You needn't get upset over ridding the world of a skunk like that.'

'I'm not grieving for his worthless hide,' Jim jeered at himself. 'I've killed for less in the past, and felt no worse over it. Daresay I could have killed the boy as well, and still felt nothing. I used to pretend I shot men down for a cause, justice even, but the sad truth is I enjoyed it, and it's become a habit.'

'Drinking won't help.'

'That what you tell your whores?' His eyes rested briefly on the supple curves of Lil, still hanging around hopefully in case her boss relented.

Maggie's uneasy glance took in the girl's restless manner and his clear inclinations. 'It's your funeral, Jim. She's no good for you, nor any of her kind.'

'No need to take that risk,' he agreed easily. 'The bottle's all I need for now.'

Maggie drifted smoothly away when he turned his attention back to the glass in front of him, aware that he'd snubbed her. She didn't blame him, more than enough of her customers did the same when they weren't feeling sorry for themselves.

'Bar-keep,' he yelled, throwing the measure in front of him down his throat. 'Bring me the bottle.'

'He's all yours,' Maggie told the shadowing Lil shortly, who giggled prettily. 'But don't do anything silly, or try to cross him; he's a dangerous man, even for a pretty girl like you.'

Lil giggled again with the contemptuous arrogance of youth, and flounced off to the bar. Maggie's lips tightened angrily, but she didn't act on her impulse to discipline the girl.

'You'll learn for yourself one day,' she murmured softly under her breath.

Several drinks passed before Jim took any real notice of the girl at his side. He vaguely realized that he'd been buying for her while she prattled merrily away, talking of this and that; none of which he'd taken the least heed to.

'You'd better take me upstairs before you fall over,' she decided at last, eyeing his unsteady slouch with some dismay. 'You sure are laying one on tonight.'

Jim nodded. A bed would be fine, so long as there was a bottle to hand. He slipped one arm around her slim waist, and signalled for a drink with the other. The flesh under his hand felt soft and yielding, she'd do, if only she weren't so garrulous. Increasingly aware that the room was beginning to spin, he allowed himself to be led up the narrow staircase and into a small room, furnished with a low-lying cot, and precious little else.

He flopped onto the coverlet, while she shook off her shoes, and began to fiddle with the laces down her back.

'Here, you help,' she murmured, hoping to incite his lust with the provocative offer.

But he'd already begun to snore.

'Jim. Wake up, damn you.'

The gambler groaned under the violent grip of the hands that shook him, and peered blearily into Maggie's face.

'I was rude to you,' he admitted at once. 'I shouldn't have spoke that way; ought to have saved the recriminations for myself.' He sat up wondering and held his aching head. 'Where's the girl gone? Is it morning already?'

'No.' Maggie held out his pocket-book. 'I took it off the little trollop. You'd only been up here a minute or two before she was down again, grinning like a cat that's stole the cream from under the dairy-maid's nose. Seemed downright odd to me, but when I found this, I had her whipped out on to the street.' She reached out an anxious hand towards Jim's throat. 'Your diamond,' she hissed. 'I thought the little bitch took it well. Don't worry, we'll get it back soon enough. Silas!' She called out a strident summons to the tall, thickset man hovering by the door with a stout cudgel in his hands. 'Get after the hussy, and give her another taste of your cane.'

'No need,' Jim interfered wearily. 'That particular gem never brought me any luck, nor its last owner.' He rose. 'I'd better leave now, I'm not fit company for a woman.' Nor anyone else, he acknowledged bitterly to himself.

He strode into the night giving little or no thought to his direction, only half aware from the size and grandeur of the houses that he'd strayed into one of the more fashionable districts of town. A rattling and scraping from above caught at his ears.

'God damn me.' He rubbed his eyes and looked up again, his mouth hanging open foolishly.

A slim youth was edging gingerly out of a garret window, high above the street, a makeshift rope made of some bedding material in his hands. Jim stepped back into the shadows and watched as the drama began to unfold.

The lad dropped his load and tried to peer down at its length. The gambler could have told him that it ended several feet above the ground, but the youngster daren't lean out far enough to see this clearly for himself; instead he began to climb down, pressing his feet against the wall while he clung to the sheets. This tenuous form of support ended abruptly, and with a swiftly stifled shriek of alarm, the boy found himself swinging helplessly at the end of his rope.

Jim darted forward, clearing the low wall that separated him from the house with a single bound. He grinned, feeling more alive than he'd done for months, and caught the boy's slight weight when he dropped. For an instant he goggled at the bundle in his arms, and abruptly dropped the slim figure.

'What the hell?' He caught himself, and bowed slightly, his skin still tingling from the soft weight of her breasts, where they'd crushed hard against his chest.

'Your servant, ma'am.' He grinned again at the dismay evident in her face, guessing she was a servant girl absconding with some knick-knack of her mistress's.

'You'll help me.' The voice was cultured, and despite its plaintive tone, well used to command. She was no servant, but nevertheless intended an escape, unless he missed his mark.

'If you require it,' he answered on a whim, warming to the girl's impudence. Privately he considered she should be returned to her parents, but he felt a curious reluctance to do so. A sudden apprehension struck him. 'You're not eloping?'

'Just the opposite,' she returned airily, her eyes searching up and down the street. 'It's too light out here. Those trees will provide cover.' She pointed out a dark, shadowed copse, and moving lightly on her feet, swiftly gained their shelter, surprisingly agile for one of her sex.

'You're drunk,' she observed dispassionately when he finally joined her under the shadows of an old oak tree.

'Yes,' he agreed gravely.

'Is that why you dropped me?' There was a hint of reproach in her face, and an endearing sense of innocence.

'Probably,' he agreed with a nice sense of tact. 'But I promise not to do so again.' His eyebrows shot up quizzically. 'I gather you're trying to run away.'

'From my uncle,' she confided in him. 'He wants to force me into a marriage with his son.'

'You don't like him?'

'He's fat, with a wet mouth.'

'I see,' returned Jim. In his present state of inebriation it seemed perfectly natural that this disqualification of her cousin's right to husbandhood should result in a high-spirited young girl escaping into the night. 'Where do you intend to go?'

'My father's partner lives in San Francisco. If you could escort me to the railway station, I'll make my own way to his protection. How much do you think it will cost?' The girl pulled an intricately decorated purse from the depths of her costume and began to count out her small store of coins.

'More than that,' decided Jim. He might be drunk, but that didn't disqualify him from calculating the cost of a trip across half the continent.

'Oh.' She looked defeated, but set her face in a mulish expression. 'I'll have to earn the rest during the journey.'

'What can you do?'

'Nothing,' replied the girl ingenuously, 'but I'll learn.'

'I'll help you.' The unexpected offer surprised Jim more than it did the girl. It's your penance, he told himself but, to his surprise, he found himself looking forward to the task. The chit was pretty enough, fresh faced with wide, emerald-green eyes that peered with candid sincerity over high set cheeks, with the faintest tinge of pink washing into her face under his scrutiny. Unabashed by her discomfiture, he dropped his gaze to study her figure more closely; slim it may be, but not under-developed.

'Where did you find those clothes?'

'My dresser's young nephew.' She was still blushing under his steadily appraising gaze.

'He's smaller than you,' Jim decided with the candour of the very drunk, unaware that his observation could only serve to disconcert her further. 'Much smaller.'

Vaguely concerned by the problem, he wondered how he'd ever come to mistake her sex.

2
RAILROAD CHASE

Next morning, Jim Delaney's thoughts hung in a curious limbo between waking and drowsy unconsciousness. He was in bed, wasn't he? Then why wasn't he lying down? His fingers stretched out shakily, and immediately retreated. Someone was sharing the bed with him. Were they sitting up too? He tried to apply his mind to the problem, stubbornly ignoring its refusal to co-operate.

His head hurt, and there was an annoying rattle from the rails when the carriage moved over them. The thought struck hard; he was on a moving train. His eyelids fluttered briefly open, and immediately closed again, blotting out the unseasonably bright glare of the morning sun which shone through a wide expanse of window.

He groaned, convinced of his fate. He was riding the railroad.

'My uncle's very tired. I believe he stayed up most

of the night.'

Jim's bleary eyes fixed on the youngster by his side, memories of the previous night flooding back in a wild, unbelievable rush.

A burst of laughter from a coarse-faced drummer seated opposite greeted the youngster's pronouncement, its harsh bark accompanied by a disdainful sniff from the buxom matron by the window.

'I reckon you're right there, son,' the salesman sniggered. 'Your uncle stayed up late, so's he could hang one on.' He laughed loud and long at his own humour.

'He's really very sober in the general way.' The lad's ingenuous speech elicited a fresh burst of merriment from the drummer, and a grunt of protest from the woman.

'How old are you?' She couched her question in the type of censorious tone that invoked cold prickles down the gambler's spine.

'Well....'

'Sixteen, and well able to take care of himself,' Jim spoke firmly. His head still hurt, but he was wide awake, and possessed of a lively fear that the woman suspected him of some clandestine purpose. If only she knew! The whiskey fumes continued to clear from his head while he stared her down.

'Thank the Lord you're awake, Uncle.' A faintly effeminate tone in the girl's voice made the gambler wince. He ran his eyes swiftly over her slim form, trying to convince himself she'd pass for a lad, despite the overwhelming evidence that she'd already suc-

ceeded in doing so. The overly large jacket worn over
a loose shirt, both of which she'd borrowed from his
wardrobe, effectively disguised her figure, and he
closed his eyes again in palpable relief.

'Yes.' Jim slipped into a monosyllabic melancholy
while the mists continued to roll back. 'I'm awake.'
He groaned again while he ran over the main points
of the night's events.

'Come on,' he commanded peremptorily. 'I'm
going to need some exercise before breakfast.' The
gambler rose abruptly, and grasping the girl's arm,
began to propel her down the car, cursing the surrounding mass of passengers under his breath.
'Damn it, is there nowhere private we can talk?'

'The sleeping car,' she replied demurely, shaking
off his grip. 'You booked couches for us, though we
never got to occupy them.' She stared at him
reproachfully. 'You snore, too. I didn't get a wink of
sleep once you collapsed into that seat.'

Jim regarded her nonplussed, but wisely refused to
be drawn, simply turning about to march down the
length of the train.

'Don't mince,' he warned shortly. 'A lad your age
strides out.'

She nodded, and dutifully lengthened her stride.

As the girl had suspected, the sleeping car was large-
ly empty, its wide couches, either side of the central
gangway, generally visible through the open curtains
that surrounded them. They sat down together on a
lower berth while the gambler stared at her afresh.

'I don't even know your name.'

'My parents christened me Catherine Elizabeth O'Brien, but you may call me Cat.' She nodded with a satisfied smirk. 'The name suits a boy well enough.'

'James Elgood Delaney.' Jim returned the introduction with a slight bow, fighting against an urge to hold out his hand in the formal manner. Despite the simple, homespun garments she'd borrowed, the girl's manner was assured, even regal, and he began to form the opinion she was older than he'd first suspected. Her fresh-faced innocence, beheld in the sober light of day, held a poised sense of composure inconsistent with the very young. In her early twenties, perhaps? Somewhat surprising then, that she should seek to escape marriage to her cousin in such a clandestine manner. Why couldn't she simply refuse him?

'I already know your name,' she surprised him. 'You were quite talkative last night.'

'I was?' he questioned warily. He wondered what he'd been talkative about.

'Oh yes. The hotel porter consulted the timetable for us, and when we found there was no suitable train for several hours, we sat in your room and made an attempt at conversation. You weren't very coherent, but I gather you'd recently killed someone.'

He pursed his lips angrily. 'I'm a damned fool.'

'I wouldn't say that, Mr Delaney,' she replied coolly. 'It sounded as if your victim were better dead, and at least you had the decency to leave the room while

I donned your clothing.' She grinned cheekily. 'No mean feat in your condition.'

'My friends call me Jim,' he offered gently.

'Thank you, I'd like to be your friend.' She lowered her gaze bashfully. 'But I'd prefer to call you Uncle James, if you don't mind?' She smiled up at him, a delightful dimple forming in her cheeks. 'While we're on the train, at least.'

A note of doubt crept into his mind, fuelled by the hesitation evident in her final words.

'You're not proposing to leave the train, are you?'

'I hope you intend to remain sober until we reach San Francisco.' She studiously avoided the point at issue. 'I collect that you don't need my money, but my father's partner will be pleased to reimburse you for any expenses incurred on my behalf.'

'You're right, I don't need your money,' he replied flatly, staring at her innocent expression with suspicion bright in his eyes. 'Does your father really have a partner in San Francisco?'

'Yes, of course.' She blushed under his query. 'Or at least, he did until he died. My father, that is. His share of the business is held in a trust which allows me a regular income.'

The gambler let the posthumous nature of the partnership pass. 'Then what are you worried about?'

'My uncle is a dangerous man.'

Jim frowned uneasily. 'We've left him far behind. Why should he suspect you're travelling on this particular train? Or in this direction at all, come to that?'

'I have no other relatives in the United States.

Where else would I go, but west?'

It was an evasive answer as Jim well recognised. Did she have relatives in another country? Whatever the answer to that, San Francisco was merely a staging post on her journey, he decided, and her father's partner, even if he existed, provided as a sop to his own curiosity. He tried again.

'Your uncle's playing the fool if he chases an unwilling bride for his son.'

'I'm an heiress.'

'Even so....'

'He plans to kidnap me.'

Jim decided then that Catherine must be the victim of an over-imaginative mind if she really believed her uncle would chase an unwilling bride across the entire country. More than likely, he was still unaware she'd absconded during the night, and bearing in mind their long head start, there was little or no chance of him catching up with them. The question of what to do next could be safely be left until they reached San Francisco. Catherine would have to confide in him there. He grimaced, uncomfortably aware in his own mind, that he'd already committed himself further than absolutely necessary.

'I need some air,' he decided suddenly, sensing the change in pace as the engineer began to brake. He peered out of the window. 'We may be able to buy coffee when we stop.'

But it was only a simple halt, and the hut that served as a station building was deserted.

As soon as the train drew to a halt, Jim climbed

down, turning the problem over in his mind, and watching with desultory interest the activities of the crew taking on water. While they waited, a couple of horsemen rode up, and boarded the train. A moment later the whistle sounded, and he hurriedly ascended the steps to regain the sleeping car. Catherine was nowhere in sight, and he stared around perplexed, wondering if his charge had taken the chance to escape him.

'Jim.' His name floated softly down the gangway.

'Cat,' he echoed foolishly, lowering his voice to no more than a whisper. And cursed himself for believing in the conspiracy.

'I'm here,' she answered in the same low tone. One of the curtains, pulled tight around a high couch, fluttered briefly in response to a twitch of her fingers. 'Climb up here.'

'With you?'

'Quickly, they're coming.'

Her voice was urgent enough to jerk him into action, and vaulting up, he crawled through the curtains, and on to the berth beside her. Swiftly she covered him with a convenient blanket and dived under it herself, hidden from the corridor by his bulk. The sound of heavy footsteps moved slowly down the coach.

Good God, he decided, she may be right. But how could her uncle have known where she was? A swish of curtains pulled abruptly apart came to his ears, simultaneous with a muffled curse from that berth's unsuspecting occupant.

'Can you use these guns?' Cat was pushing his bag into his hands.

'Not here,' he declared firmly, and thrust her down behind him.

Despite himself, he jumped when their own curtain was jerked back, but retained enough wit to grab the material before the compartment was flooded with light.

'Damn you,' he roared, rearing up and cracking his head painfully on the roof above.

'I'm sorry, sir.' Jim stared amazed at the figure of a lawman. 'We're looking for a girl. Probably dressed in men's clothing.'

'I'm no girl,' Jim affirmed, rubbing his eyes as though he'd just been wakened.

'No, sir. I'm sorry to trouble you.'

The marshal passed on down the car, leaving Jim to shuffle over to the edge of the bunk, uncomfortably aware of the trembling in Catherine's soft curves where she snuggled up close behind. 'They've gone,' he muttered shortly. 'And you've got some explaining to do. That was a US marshal.'

'My uncle is very influential,' she temporized. 'You won't give me up, will you?'

'No.' The gambler stared at her, but didn't ask again. She'd tell him in her own time.

Jim never did decide when it was he first felt anxious. Like many others who'd lived their life on the line, he had a sixth sense for danger, and it plucked at his mind.

The lawman had departed two days earlier, but not the companion who'd boarded with him, and the gambler wasn't altogether surprised when their train began to slow down for no apparent reason. For several hours they'd been travelling through a region of bare, scrubby desert scattered with jagged rocky outcrops, starkly illuminated by the merciless sun, blazing down from a copper sky.

He watched impassively while a band of mounted men trotted confidently up a defile close beside the railroad track.

'It's time for us to leave,' he decided at last, recognizing the train was intending to stop. And suiting action to the words, he slipped a supporting arm around Catherine's waist and thrust her out of a door on the far side of the carriage, trusting the car's bulk to hide their escape from view. They fell heavily, rolling together down a steeply sloping bank, and into the cover of some scrubby bushes. The train itself drew to a halt a short distance up the line, and the passengers found themselves paraded by its length, while the band of masked outlaws examined them. It may have been a simple robbery, but to Jim's mind, far too much attention was directed at its more youthful passengers.

'Do you believe me now?'

Jim nodded. 'That your uncle wants you, yes. But there's more to your story than that.' He watched her face suspiciously.

'Like I said, I'm an heiress.'

'Catherine Elizabeth O'Brien,' he queried. 'An

Irish heiress? You don't look Irish, and you don't have a trace of the brogue in your voice. Is that your real name?'

'Oh yes,' she answered easily. 'My father was of Irish extraction. He was a cavalry officer in the French Army, assigned as personal escort to my mother during a state visit to France. They fell in love over the space of a few weeks, and married secretly rather than allow her to return to Russia. It cost him his commission when they were forced to flee to America, but he had fortune enough to invest in a house and business. The house you caught me escaping from was theirs.'

'Where does your uncle fit into this?'

'My father died when I was quite young, and my mother more recently. They left me a respectable inheritance, but I had no idea I was an heiress until a couple of days ago, when Uncle Boris came to visit with his son. He's not really my uncle you know, more like second cousin, but he introduces himself as such. He took over the house, and elected to act as my guardian, effectively imprisoning me. It was easy for him, he's a diplomat with considerable power and influence, even in this country.'

'Why now?'

'My mother had taken care to hide herself, but as a countess closely related to a royal house, it was inevitable that her death would be widely reported.'

'Then you're....'

'Yes, I'm a countess too.' She paused, and added in a small voice, 'But only if I return to Russia. The title and estates belong to the Tsar unless I claim them in person.' She stared at him. 'I would need a suitable husband to do that, of course.'

'Your cousin?' Jim's lips narrowed to a thin, murderous line. The story was beginning to fall into place.

'That's correct. It would be he who benefited from the arrangement, of course. A woman's wealth passes to her husband's control, and I should end my days as an effective prisoner at court, while he remained free to do as he wished.'

'But without him, you have nothing?'

'I have the house and an income from my father's business; plus, as I learned so recently, an estate in Alaska inherited from my mother's side. It's part of America now, safe from my uncle unless he can force me to marry his son.'

'I can see him chasing you for wealth and position in the Russias, but not for some barren Alaskan estate.'

'There is gold reported there,' she reminded him simply. 'In Russia there would only be position. The estates, though vast, are not particularly rich. And a courtier laden with Alaskan gold might more easily reconcile the Tsar to the loss of lands he may well wish to retain.'

'Hush.' Jim silenced the girl with a gesture. 'The train's leaving.'

Together they watched their erstwhile transport steam into the distance, leaving the bunch of riders behind. Soon, they too, had turned their horses and disappeared.

'What now? I assume you have some plan.' Catherine turned wide eyes on her saviour, confident he'd know what to do next. James Delaney was, she considered, a resourceful man.

'We'll wait the day out here,' he answered shortly, his eyes busily searching out cover from the burning sun. 'It'll be easier to walk in the dark. Safer too, I've no doubt.'

3

THE SHARPSHOOTER

'Get down.' The moon was up, and they'd been
trekking most of the night when Jim Delaney issued
his peremptory command. He dropped into a prone
position, partly shielded by a hummock of earth
close by the rail track, and pulled the girl down
beside him.

Catherine, unused to walking for such long peri-
ods, was too tired to do any more than lie on the
ground at her protector's side, grateful for any
respite from the gruelling pace he'd set, however
brief in duration.

A clatter of hooves disturbed the silence of the
night, leading the gambler to narrow his eyes along
the track. More than one horse, he decided, then
swore under his breath when the figure of a tall, thin
rider loomed into view, sitting one mount, and leading a further pair. He remained still while the horses
stepped carefully forward, following the line of the

track just as they themselves had, but from the opposite direction.

'I'm a friend.' The voice was deep, confident
enough of their position to rein in and speak quietly.

'Don't move, friend.' Jim raised himself warily on
his haunches. 'I have you covered.'

The other laughed softly. 'I raided your bag, where
you concealed your guns. I don't suppose you have
another weapon.' A bulky bundle spun from the
other's hand and dropped at Jim's feet. The heavy
leather holster shimmered dully under the moon's
waning light. His gun lay sheathed in its protection.

Jim gave up. He laid a hand lightly on Catherine's
shoulder, warning her to silence, and stood up to
face his tracker.

'You know a good deal about me.' The simple
statement concealed a question, and the other knew
it.

'You're Diamond Jim Delaney, gambler and sometime lawman. The legend I knew of, but I never saw
you in the flesh until the other night when you killed
a man over a game of cards. Your name was on everyone's lips, but I asked the barman to be sure; he
seemed to know your reputation. Pure luck we were
on the train together. I didn't expect our paths to
cross again so soon, but I was fortunate enough to
spot your escape from the outlaw gang.' He grinned
reminiscently. 'You leapt off the train moments
before it was brought to a halt by their ambush. Was
it you they were after? Or the lad?'

'And you? Which are you after?' Jim ignored the

question of Catherine's sex. If the stranger knew she were a woman, he'd betray himself soon enough.

'You're the one who interests me, unless the lad can shoot as well. I'm known to my audiences as Mountain Boy Pym; John to those I choose as friends. As to my business, I run a small show demonstrating aspects of the wild and woolly West to a crowd of gawking spectators. We get to travel a lot, but it's a precarious living at best.' Pym's speech held a touch of the showman about it, and Jim grunted.

'This we you're talking about, are they on the train too?'

'My fellow artistes are resting in town, waiting for us; ten, twelve miles away.' He shrugged, pointed towards the rapidly waning moon. 'We began our tour back East but with the competition getting stiffer every day, we decided to move on with the spring.' He looked puzzled. 'Where is the boy?'

Jim picked up his holster, and made a brief signal to Catherine, who rose on stiff legs to stand at his side. He buckled on the belt, and swiftly checked the gun; it was loaded.

'How'd you know where to look for us?'

'You had to be along the railroad track some-where,' explained the scout. 'No other trail for miles, less'n to the outlaws' hide-out. So I followed the rails myself, and waited way up on that bluff yonder. When you came into sight, I marked your position, and calculated where you'd be when I came up with you.' He smiled easily. 'No problem, I really was a mountain man once. Had to track for my life in those days.'

'Why?'

John Pym didn't attempt to misunderstand the gambler's question. 'I need your skill with the gun. My own sharpshooter left us last week, said he preferred to stay in the East. He'd grown too big for his boots in any case; became a menace to us all, always pushing quarrels. He really came to believe in his own publicity, that his was the fastest draw west of the Pecos.'

'And is it?'

'Could be,' Pym nodded. 'He's the fastest man I've seen in a long while, and I've seen a few in my time. You'd run him close, though.'

'Where did you say you were heading with the show?'

'Out West. I hear there's a surprising popularity for such shows that way. Possibly as far as San Francisco, if I can get the bookings.' Pym studied the gambler's face carefully, evidently fully aware of their eventual destination.

'We'll join you,' decided Catherine immediately. She'd been standing quietly at Jim's side, but, ever watchful, he'd noted the occasional sideward glances the old man had given her. He stared at her himself, and cursed. The night had been close, and she'd discarded the bulky jacket, leaving her clad in a shirt that clung damply to the perspiration on her body, and plainly proclaimed her sex.

'That's not a problem, we have women with the show.' John Pym had seen his dilemma. He slid from his horse and executed a small bow. 'Do you ride, ma'am?'

'No.'

'Of course I do.' Catherine ignored Jim's swiftly barked interjection. 'Bareback, if necessary.' She'd been taken to see shows of this sort herself, and knew what would be expected of her.

'Damn it, Cat. It's not right for you to wear that skirt.' Jim glared angrily at Catherine's costume for the first act. She was made up in a deerskin dress, in imitation of an Indian maiden, and her face flushed brick red under his flare of disapproval.

'You don't like it?'

'It's not that,' he started, beginning to wonder what he did mean. They'd been with the show for several days, rehearsing for their first performance, time in which he'd got to know her better. But now he was forced to think of her as a woman, perhaps for the first time.

Even he had to admit that her slim figure suited the dress, which hugged the contours of her firm, high-tilted breasts and hard, flat stomach to flare out across her hips, and end shockingly short, just above her knees. She had lovely legs too; long and slender, their velvet skin so incredibly smooth. He bit his lip, and spat out an oath under his breath; tasting the instinctive reaction to desire when he considered how good she must feel to touch.

Something of his thoughts must have been evident to her senses too, for without warning she leaned for-

ward in swift response, laying her cool lips briefly on
his.

'I'll be all right,' she confided, and skipped back
quickly, out of his reach.

'You're on, Jim.'

Any further reaction on his part was as suddenly
forestalled. One of the other girls, dressed in a similar manner to Catherine, had called from the
entrance to the ring where Mountain Boy Pym was
roaring out his introduction.

The ring itself was simply a half circle of barren
land, surrounded by low laid planks, set to keep the
audience back, and, at a further distance, roped off
to provide a wide enclosure only paying customers
could enter. His entrance was made through a wide
swathe of canvas, roughly painted to depict a desert
scene, and erected to provide some sort of background for the acts to come.

He walked on, half crouched in parody of a gun-
fighter's favourite stance, feeling more foolish than
dangerous, but the roars of approval soon stripped
the layers of reserve from his character, and he
entered into the spirit of the act. He drew and fired,
twirling his gun and firing again, confident that the
shots were blanks, especially loaded for the performance. Real bullets would have been too dangerous
for exploits such as this.

Pym was still bellowing out his monologue on a
variety of famous gunfighters he'd known, when Jim
began his finale in a showy display of dazzling skill;
diving for the ground, rolling under the fence, and

firing from the hip amidst a crowd of enthusiastic
youngsters, who split like a covey of prairie partridges
from his snarling presence. A last dangerous scowl in
their direction, and he leapt back into the ring,
thankful that Pym had the foresight to provide him
with a script to follow.

The final applause had barely died down before
he reloaded; real bullets this time, for target practise.
The targets were wooden discs, small enough to
appear a difficult shot from the depths of the audience, but thrown close enough by the ringmaster for
his own ease. Jim's innate accuracy with his pistol had
been honed by constant practise, and target after target split through from his draw and shoot tactics. He
bowed gracefully, and made his exit amidst the roar
of approval, more apprehensive of the sharp shooting with a rifle, to follow some time later in the show.

The next act was a tableaux of sorts. Indians, a
scant few of them real, began to trail onto centre
stage, their weary ponies drawing the materials needed to make up tepees, and while they completed
their work, three Indian maidens rode bareback to
continue the entertainment.

The centre-point of the act was a girl of real talent.
As skimpily clothed as the rest of her entourage, she
performed her horse-back acrobatics with no hint of
embarrassment, though her skirt continually swirled
back to reveal the figure beneath. Jim applauded as
loud as anyone, but narrowed his eyes when
Catherine joined in, performing a complicated routine that involved her leaping on and off the moving

ponies. Bare-legged, and riding bareback, he was annoyed to find she was displaying her thighs to every man in the tent.

So what, he jeered at himself. Damn it, was he beginning to care for the girl? He shrugged, uneasily aware that he was, and settled down in a vain attempt to enjoy the display.

The soft flooding light of evening wafted over the pair as they sat beside the stream, dangling their feet in the cool waters, following their latest performance. They'd been on the move for a couple of weeks, playing to a different audience each night, and were now encamped on the outskirts of a larger town than usual. Both of them looked forward to a well-earned break from the gruelling routine and constant pressure of the shows.

'One more night,' their leader had assured his exhausted troupe, 'and we'll take a few days' rest, before heading down to Wichita.'

'We'll have to leave the show,' Jim told the girl earnestly, his bare chest glowing pale gold in the deepening twilight. 'We'll never get to San Francisco at the rate we're moving.'

'What about John? How will he replace you?' Catherine displayed a curious reluctance to move on. Her thoughts contemplated a dull, conventional future and, moreover, a future without Jim and the excitement of performing.

'That's his problem.' Jim stared at the smooth perfection of her thighs, bare where the buckskin dress had been peeled back to permit her to sit by the water. He'd got used to watching her perform in skimpy costumes, but not to sitting so close that the scent of her invaded his nostrils with its warm invitation

'What do you wear under that?' The question was almost involuntary, but the answer had troubled him ever since he'd first spotted her in the short skirt, especially when he considered that those clients sitting close by the ring must command far more spectacular views than he did from its entrance. It would be nothing very concealing, he suspected, knowing that Pym considered the showgirls' scanty clothing to bring in as many customers as the skill of its acts.

'Wouldn't you like to know,' she teased, and laying a hand on her hem, pretended to lift it higher.

Jim turned away, clenching his fists in sudden arousal. He'd had many women in his life, but Catherine was different. A swift roll under the stars wouldn't be enough, and a lady like her could never completely be his. He felt her gentle fingers light on his shoulders, and the soft thrust of her breasts on his bare back. Her hair rustled silkily against his cheeks when she rose on to her knees and nuzzled tenderly at the side of his neck, the sharp flick of her tongue relishing the texture of his skin.

Wondering afresh, he turned slowly, his face eagerly tilting to taste her lips, while his hands sought to span her trim waist. For a long, slow moment she gazed into his eyes as though to calculate his intentions, then dipped her head to their first, precious kiss. His hands moved to shape the bowed ridge of her back, drawing her closer on to his waiting lap, in an ever deepening embrace. She responded immediately, kissing him back with an ardour that surprised him in one so innocent, her lips parting readily beneath his plundering mouth in loving surrender. Their tongues fenced, flickering intimately, while her arms entwined ever tighter about his neck, her long, supple fingers delving deep into the thicker hair at his nape. Lost to the knowledge of her in his arms, Jim freed one hand to explore the intricate weave of her ribs, and trace the burgeoning outline of one small breast in fluttering wonder. Prey to the same burning desires as himself, Catherine threw back her head in wanton abandon, arching gleefully while she exposed the softly scented hollows of her throat to his ravaging hunger.

The rattle of stones was John Pym's method of interrupting them tactfully, Jim realized; the mountain man seldom made a sound when he moved. He swiftly released the girl, who, having jerked the deerskin skirt down to cover her thighs, stumbled to her feet abashed.

'A warning, Jim.'

'A warning?' For a moment Jim thought his boss was warning him against making love to Catherine.

'I'm sorry if I chose my moment badly, but I had to tell you sometime. Nathan Kelly is in town, and primed to cause trouble.'

'Your old sharpshooter,' Jim guessed.

'As you say. I doubt if he's set to cause a ruckus

during the show, but it might be as well if you didn't hang around town during the day.'

'I seldom do, John.'

'He'll be watching for you.' The old mountain man studied Jim, 'but no one could blame you for avoiding him.'

'I won't do that either.' Jim maintained a stubborn refusal to run scared. 'He wants to find me bad enough, I'll be here.'

John nodded, and turned on his heels, swiftly disappearing into the gathering gloom.

'You're right, we'll leave tonight.' Catherine stepped close to him, pressing the length of her body into his, but the moment had passed, and he gently disentangled himself.

'We'll perform one last show, Cat.' Jim's voice sounded weary. 'We owe that much to the company; it'll give John a chance to find our replacements during the break. I'll head into town and buy tickets for the train tomorrow.'

'What about Nathan Kelly?' Catherine's face reflected the fear she felt for his safety.

'He won't be waiting at the station,' Jim laughed. 'Down by the saloon, most like.'

'Be careful.'

Jim clasped her hand in his, and led her back to their camp, where she shared a wagon with the other unmarried women. He nodded quietly. 'I'll be careful.'

Jim was correct in assuming Nathan Kelly wouldn't wait

for him at the station. The erstwhile sharpshooter had
elected instead to visit the camp in a studied and
deliberate challenge to his replacement.

'Howdy champ,' Kelly greeted the gambler with a
wide smile of welcome when he returned from his
business, but a malignant glint from the depths of his
eyes belied the false bonhomie. 'I hear tell you're
almost as good as me with a pistol.'

'Likely so.' Jim glanced around the uncomfortable
huddle of performers present, thankful Catherine
wasn't numbered amongst them.

'Like to try a few shots with me?' The gunman
nonchalantly tossed one of the broad disks into the
air, drew and picked it off with contemptuous ease.

'I do that every night,' Jim reminded the man.

'Then it should be easy.' Nathan Kelly grinned
nastily. 'Shall we make your girlfriend the prize?'

The pieces slotted into place at once. Kelly was
there for a purpose, his presence no longer the
unfortunate accident that Pym had suspected. Uncle
Boris, or so the gambler presumed, had located the
girl, perhaps even watched her perform. The gunman was a convenient pawn to bait Jim Delaney,
holding him in place until Catherine could be
abducted. And it was only Nathan Kelly's arrogance
in alerting the gambler that looked set to foil the
plan; Jim measured the odds and began his draw
immediately.

The other's reply was lightning fast, but Jim's
razor-sharp reflexes had been tested under combat
many a time, and his pistol exploded a moment

before Kelly's, cutting the gunman down before he was properly set. The reply, instinctively triggered after he'd already been hit, ploughed into the ground close by the gambler's feet.

'Where's Catherine?' Jim rushed forward to kick away his opponent's gun, while he stared wildly around the camp.

His cry of alarm was swiftly answered amongst the troupe.

'We ain't seen her for a while,' one of the girls affirmed with puzzled stare. 'She must have gone into town or she'd be here, what with all the shooting.'

A train whistle blew loud from the other side of town, and Jim Delaney cursed roundly.

'Where're they taking her?' he menaced the fallen gunman.

Kelly moaned in pain, holding his side, and Jim kicked him viciously, impervious to any suggestion of pity.

'The man asked you a question.' A large knife appeared at Kelly's throat when John Pym suddenly materialized to repeat Jim's request for information. 'It ain't real respectful, not to reply.'

The gunman turned pale, and capitulated immediately, realizing that the mountain man was in no mood to be played with. 'San Francisco. Gonna take a packet to Alaska.'

'Why?' The mountain man allowed his blade to slip a fraction of an inch, drawing blood. He intended to milk the limits of Nathan Kelly's information.

'I don't know. Please, I'm telling the truth.' The unfortunate gunman screamed when Pym deliberately applied his knife again, slicing deeper into the bloodied flesh.

'No need, John. I can guess the rest.'

Jim swiftly surveyed what little Catherine had known about her uncle's plans. They'd head for Alaska, as Kelly had suggested, the goldfields in all probability. And from there, travel overland to the Bering Straits, where they'd find men willing to transport them across that narrow channel to the safety of the Russian Empire, and the court of the Tsar himself.

He made a silent vow to follow them, even so far as the throne room, if needs be.

4

SEA VOYAGE

Jim Delaney finally arrived in San Francisco nearly a week later, following a marathon journey across country by train. Shocked at first by the myriad of vessels preparing to sail for Alaska, he soon realized that while gold fever was at its height, any vessel capable of floating would be pressed into service, ship-shape or not. Despite the immense distances involved, plenty of people seemed willing to take the risk of travelling on some old scow that might not survive the perilous journey, a sentiment he soon began to share.

A brief call at the shipping company offices, jostling through an ill tempered crowd of others bent on similar missions, was enough to show him that buying a ticket for immediate departure was no longer feasible. Any reputable company had filled their lists for months in advance, and there seemed no hope of his setting sail in the short term.

Further doubts crowded through his mind. How influential was Uncle Boris? A diplomat, and most probably a nobleman too, he'd have access to channels denied the ordinary traveller. Jim swiftly guessed that this position, coupled with the greasing of a few palms, would allow the Russian party to gain an earlier passage than himself.

One obvious opportunity to inaugurate his own journey soon occurred to the gambler's agile mind, and he set about putting his plan into immediate effect. Several hours invested in searching the dockyard stews and bar-rooms finally bore fruit. He located an officer of one of the better companies who was susceptible to bribery, and bearing the not inconsiderable financial outlay with aplomb, he bought himself a post in the stoke-room of the steamer *American Fidelity*, a larger and more luxurious ship than most of those setting out for Alaska. It was the type of ship, he convinced himself eagerly, that an influential Russian diplomat might well use himself, and one, moreover, that promised the pace to make up lost time should the Russian party have already left. His only regret was that he'd been forced to board immediately, unable to restock his meagre fund of cash with the money he'd cabled for on first entering the city.

He stood on the tiny, part-enclosed, rear deck that, as a stoker, formed his only access to the outside world, and gazed out at the early morning bustle on the quay. They were already fired up to leave with the tide later that morning and his own shift would soon be at work, stoking the huge fires that fed the ship's engines. Despite the fact that he hadn't yet been put to work in earnest, he was already stained with a stoker's grime, the grit invading the cramped quarters he shared with dozens of others deep in the stern of the ship.

A brief spate of activity surged around the quay, under the bows of the steamer, and Jim strained out to investigate. A carriage had arrived and its occupants were engaged on boarding ship. Grinding his teeth, he could only watch from afar as a heavily veiled woman, confined to a chair, was wheeled across the gang-plank by what appeared to be a nurse, closely followed by two gentlemen, fawned over by an officer. He couldn't be certain, but his gambler's instincts told him it could only be the party he was chasing. Even from a distance he could see the woman's head lolling loosely, perhaps heavily drugged to keep her quiet, an obvious precaution for Uncle Boris to take. A bell rang in the depths below, and he realised he was being called to work.

That work as a stoker would incur certain disadvantages for a man who wished to roam the ship at will had already occurred to the gambler. The reality was far worse than he'd imagined.

The work itself was physically demanding in a way he could hardly believe. Trapped in the depths of the ship, with only the satanic glare of the fires to light the dust-laden, grimy atmosphere, he laboured stripped to the waist against the suffocating heat, his aching muscles straining to shift the jagged chunks of coal. And when the gates were opened, a choking mass of ash, and superheated air would sear his lungs, frizzling the hair on his chest, while he laboured to fill its cavernous maw with more of the jet-black fuel.

Their mess was hardly in better shape; with inadequate cleaning facilities, and exhaustion etched into their faces, the men of his shift threw themselves into their cots, spreading their muck about regardless. In such brutal conditions Jim carried his small store of cash upon his person, but remained fearful for the safety of the rest of his belongings, amongst them his pistol. But he soon found that stealing from shipmates was a sin which carried instant retribution. A kangaroo court was swiftly assembled to deal with the first such outrage, and sadistic pleasure taken in the administration of the sentence. Neither the bloodied victim, nor any other was likely to repeat the crime.

He soon found that most of the ship was out of bounds to stokers. He'd fully expected the passenger's quarters to be denied him, but naively assumed he'd have the run of the rest of the ship during the long reaches of night. Any prospect of that was soon quashed, and the possibility of disguise rendered meaningless by his constantly blackened face and clothing. Imprisoned in the stoke holds, he couldn't even attempt to communicate with a steward who might have been bribed to do his work for him. Regretfully, he gave up all thoughts of communication with Catherine during the voyage, and saved his

energies for their arrival at the port of Skagway, gate-
way to the great Alaskan heartland.

Night and day made little difference to the enduring
monotony and exhaustion Jim suffered during the
first stages of the voyage. Strong and fit as he'd kept
himself, the constant back-breaking exercise with a
shovel over long watches combined to take its toll on
his physical reserves, but by the time they reached
more northern latitudes, he'd long since sloughed
off any lingering remnants of a more sedentary life.
Quietly confident, he stood ready to face the future
with an enthusiasm and stamina at odds with many of
his fellows.

  He'd already planned his next moves: shore leave
at Skagway with a mission to locate and free
Catherine from her captors; followed by a tri-
umphant return to the ship, this time as a favoured
passenger. With a constant stream of vessels plying
their trade to the port, there would surely be no
shortage of berths on the homeward voyage.

  The final day of their travels loomed large. Jim
already knew they were close to their destination, a
brief view of snowy hill-tops and forested valleys from
the small rear deck had convinced him of that, but a
brutal day in the coal holds robbed him of the ability to recognize their manoeuvrings in the bay. Off
duty at last, he finally realised they'd hove to only by
the expressions of joy on the faces of his companions. Like many of the others, Jim prepared to go
ashore.

Even a thorough wash failed to remove the ingrained coal dust from his face and body, but his spirits remained high until he re-entered the mess room to pack his kit for the last time. The enthusiastic raillery had disappeared, replaced by an ugly, sullen silence that shook the gambler's nerve.

'What is it?' Jim spoke to one of the older hands, a veteran of hundreds of voyages, but one who'd planned to desert this trip, eager for the chance of a share in the golden harvest.

'Ah lad, the captain's a downy one, an' no mistake. We're all locked in. Likely the whole crew of us. Got a few trusted men, and he's armed them. Even if we break through the locks, they'll stop us.' The man sighed, as though resigning himself to another voyage.

'But, why?'

He was led to a grimy porthole, and shown the view. The cold, choppy waters of the inlet upon which Skagway was situated, lay covered in an endless vista of ships, the vast bulk of them presenting a ghostly, deserted appearance.

'Abandoned.' His new friend confirmed his view. 'The captain won't want that happening to his command. It seems that sailors are deserting at such a rate, vessels are stuck out here for months, perhaps forever, without a crew to sail them.'

Uneasily aware that it had been his own intention to desert, Jim stared around the mess. The tired, defeated faces told their own story. Many, if not all, of his companions would have taken their chance for riches in the snowy wilderness of the Alaskan hinterland. The captain was no fool to have taken such draconian precautions. He returned to his bunk and sat wrapped in thought.

He'd expected the ship to lie up against a dock for disembarkation, and under those circumstances, even an armed guard could have been circumvented. But the ship was several hundreds of yards from the motley collection of timber buildings he'd seen on the shore and, despite the brightness of an Arctic spring there was still a nip in the air. The water would be freezing, as he well knew. He was a strong swimmer, but even in the sheltered inlet, he'd be lucky to make it to shore, and it would clearly be impossible when they'd weighed anchor, and he was once again allowed on deck.

'Will we dock?' Jim continued the inquisition.

'No, mate, there's no harbour here.' His informant had been on the Alaskan run before, and knew the port well. 'Everything will be unloaded into lighters.'

'There's some trusted well enough, then?'

'The captain has to trust someone, but they'll be under armed escort, with an officer appointed to keep a watch over them.' The other eyed him carefully, and winked. 'No chance of a stoker crewing one of those boats, matey!'

Jim nodded, temporarily defeated in his chain of reasoning. He smiled. 'No harm in asking, is there?'

'You'll mark yourself as a deserter,' the older man warned him. 'May even end up in chains. Best wait awhile, I reckon.'

'What for?' Instinct told Jim that his companion had made his own plans.

'Jack Stanford,' the other thrust out his hand, deliberately making Jim wait for the information while he introduced himself. 'Been watching you a while, matey. You're no stoker, nor crew of any sort; not regular like. And you're armed.'

Jim held up a hand. 'How d'you know that?' Firearms were forbidden to the crew on pain of death, and he'd been forced to smuggle his own aboard, where he'd hidden them deep in his pack.

'I know.' Jack didn't vouchsafe any other answer, but Jim had the uneasy suspicion that the other had sorted through his belongings prior to approaching him. 'But I like the cut of your jib. You're strong enough to work hard, and ain't ever tried to shirk, far as I can see. Fact is, you always planned to desert once we reached Alaskan territory, just didn't think of the problems. I've seen all of them first hand. Got myself a roll, and bought up an old claim, too. But I need a partner.' The old sailor having broached the subject, stared at Jim expectantly.

'I didn't come for gold,' Jim told him truthfully, 'but I'd be a fool to turn down a chance at escape.'

'Sure you didn't,' agreed his new friend scornfully. He plainly didn't believe Jim Delaney's assertion. 'There's plenty for us both to share in, more if we work together.' He held out his hand again.

'How do we get out?' The gambler realized that Jack assumed the partnership was made, and didn't disabuse him. He shook hands.

'We go when the guard deserts.' Jack lowered his voice to prevent the others hearing. 'They'll release us first.'

'How do you know?'

'I hear things,' the old sailor returned mysteriously. 'It don't matter how, but the more of us is loose, the better the confusion. Makes sense really. The main body will likely rush the main deck for a boat, but we'll head for the rear. There's an overhang with the rudder beneath; give us enough purchase to hang on to until they stop searching.'

'When?'

'Not before dark, but we'll hear the outcry when it happens. The captain's nervous enough to post a guard on the guards. Reckon there'll be a fight.'

'And us?'

'We'll be hidden, just like I told you.' Jack searched the gambler's face. ' You can use that pistol of yours, I take it?'

Jim nodded silently, swiftly amending his own plans in line with the older man's thinking.

The long twilight had hardly disappeared from the sky before the sailor's warning came true. A brief scuffling above deck, barely heard in their cramped quarters, was punctuated by the louder roar of a gun. The mess came to life in a twinkling, heading for the freshly opened exit as several more shots sounded in close proximity.

'That's it, lads.' Jack was at their head, encouraging them all to break loose. The mutineers had, as he expected, released their compatriots, but the continuing bark of small arms showed that not everything was going their way.

Jim fought his way to the sailor's side, and they pressed out together, the gambler uncomfortably aware that many of the stokers were content to follow his new partner's lead rather than tackle an armed guard, but he breathed easier once they reached the open deck. Man after man leapt off the rounded stern to attempt the perilous swim, apparently unconcerned by the freezing temperatures.

'Stay with me, lad,' Jack warned, when they in turn reached the rear deck. 'That water's powerful cold, and the captain's ordered a boat to patrol.'

Jim watched the cold waters, flecked with ice ejected from the nearby river, shimmer under the lights of a lantern held on the bows of the guard boat Jack had spotted, shivering himself when several of his fellows were hauled unceremoniously from the sea. Jack had disappeared, but a moment later returned, breaking into his morbid thoughts with a light touch on his shoulder, while he displayed his booty; a length of rope and some strips of tar-soaked tarpaulin.

'Wrap your pack in this, and don't fall; it's important we remain dry,' he warned. 'The wind's already rising, and we'll be chilly enough hanging on to the rudder without wet clothing.'

'Why wait?'

The wily old sailor touched his nose in a silent gesture. 'The tide will turn in a few hours, and that makes a big difference to our chances of reaching shore. They'll be swimming against the current now, and with the water set against them, even the most powerful of swimmers will be fortunate to make it. The guard boat will collar most of them, but it's the lucky ones as will end up in the brig, those they miss will probably die of exposure. As for ourselves, we'll catch them napping later; they won't be expecting any more escapees, and the swimming will be easier.' He looped the rope around a convenient stanchion and dropped confidently over the side.

Jim followed more slowly, careful to keep out of the water. He could already feel the biting cold of its swirling eddies, and mentally agreed with the sailor. It wouldn't be easy. Negotiating the overhang to the curl of the rudder was no formality either, and he might not have made it without the support of the rope held by his new-found partner. The older man had reached their target, his slight figure hiding an agility the gambler would never have suspected, and a moment later he'd joined the old sailor in a dark corner by the rudder, supporting himself and his luggage on its vast bulk while he regained his breath.

'Quiet,' Jack commanded in a whisper while he retrieved his rope and coiled it loosely around his own tarpaulin-wrapped bundle. 'Ain't likely they'll search for us here, but you never know.'

A few hours passed, by which time Jim's circulation was beginning to slow. The air was penetratingly cold, and he was glad not to have been in the water. Without Jack's nautical knowledge, he realized he'd have swum against the tide, and probably failed to make the shore. But even his unpractised ear was able to discern the different motion of the waves swirling so close beneath.

'Keep your pack in front, and paddle quiet,' Jack demanded suddenly. 'It'll retain some air and support you. Good luck.' He lowered himself quietly into the water and began to surge slowly towards the distant shoreline. Jim followed immediately, gasping as the bitterly cold waters soaked through his clothes and attacked his skin.

5

RIVERBOAT QUEEN

Jim heard the breakers before he saw them. The cold had spread deep through his body, dulling the circulation, and numbing his senses. He grasped the insensible body of his partner and struck out, increasingly mindful that he was almost spent. A last spiteful swirl of the current carried him past the spit he was aiming for, but with a cry of relief he struck ground, and surged to his feet in a stream of freezing spray.

The loose gravel beneath his feet sought to trip him as he struggled forward, still dragging the dead weight of the old sailor, but at long last he made it to dry land. Safety, his mind told him, willing him to get to his feet. It seemed madness in the viciously cold wind, but he began to strip, first Jack and then himself, wrenching open their packs to haul on clothing kept dry by the tar-sodden tarpaulin. A low moan of pain from his partner proved the efficacy of his action.

'I'm finished, lad,' Jack bravely tried to struggle to his feet and failed, 'unless you can find shelter from this wind.'

Shelter. The one word he should have been seeking himself. Jim peered around numbly, briefly examining the bleak hinterland for any evidence of human habitation. Then, hauling Jack to his feet, began to drag him by main force along the line of the shore, praying he'd calculated their position correctly.

The following morning dawned bleak and grey, a watery sun spreading its warmth across a grateful land. A lad, little more than an infant came to milk his cow in the byre, and found them, huddled up against the warmth of the patient beast.

'Reckon you saved my life, partner.' Jack's voice was gruff, the emotion behind his words stifled by their careless inflexion.

'I'd be dead without your guidance,' Jim admitted ruefully, sorrowfully aware their partnership would have to end after the perils they'd faced together. He held out his hand.

'Oh no, you don't,' the old sailor railed, slapping the proffered hand away. 'I got the only partner I ever could trust, and you want out. How come? You got your own workings?'

'Nothing like that, Jack,' the gambler replied patiently. 'I came out here after a woman, not to dig for gold.'

'Hell, you can have any woman you want once we hit pay-dirt.'

'This one's special.' Briefly Jim filled his new friend in on Catherine's story.

'Heading for the gold-fields themselves, most likely,' mused Jack thoughtfully. 'Got money, too, have they?'

Jim nodded.

'Then they'll travel on the *Queen*, if she's still working.'

'The *Queen*?'

'Sure. She's a riverboat; about the only vessel of any size you can get across the shoals. God alone knows how they got her up here. She works a route along the river, mostly taking supplies and prospectors up to the river head. Only a couple of hundred miles, but there's a trail from there clear up to the gold-fields.' He looked crestfallen. 'Or so they say.' And in a moment of candour, apologized for his lack of first-hand knowledge. 'I've been ashore in Skagway afore but the rest is only hearsay.'

'More than I can say,' Jim shrugged. 'I'm a complete novice when it comes to this land.' He stared out at the early morning bustle in the town.

'Looks like we're partners a while longer.'

'Let's get us a hot bath, and we'll load up some gear,' agreed Jack, thoroughly relieved that the big man would be staying a while. 'You might be glad of your share in the claim yet.'

Baths were an expensive luxury in Skagway, but neither of the partners was able to resist the opportunity to wash off the residue of the coal-hole, and a few hours later they reappeared on the streets scrubbed pink, and laden with a store of the accoutrements and supplies appropriate to newly arrived prospectors for gold.

'We've still got dogs and equipment to purchase,' declared Jack, counting up their remaining coins. 'Even so, there's enough left to take ship. The *Queen* don't leave until tomorrow, so we can scout around a bit. If your lady was travelling with us on the *American Fidelity*, she can't have left Skagway yet. She'll be locked in her cabin, most like.' He slapped Jim heartily on the back, and pointed out across the makeshift harbour.

Unlike the bigger ships moored out in the bay, the riverboat drew little enough draught to pull right up to the rickety pier that fronted the bustling quay. In general format and design, she resembled the similar boats so familiar to the gambler, who'd plied his trade in their luxurious saloons all along the Mississippi and its larger tributaries, but he soon saw the differences. There was no show about this *Queen*, despite her imposing name; the paint work was neat, but unrelieved by the ornate decoration common to its more luxurious southern cousins, lending an impression of austerity to the entire ship. It was a working boat, and Jim was left in no doubt that it would form their best method of transport to the river head, and thence to the gold-fields.

'Got to pay whatever they ask,' decided Jack wisely, staggered by the price of travelling on the *Queen*.

Though he'd never attempted the perilous journey himself, he'd quizzed those who had with assiduous enthusiasm, and realised the value of the river to their journey. 'Your girl may be on board. Besides,' he added ingenuously, 'spring's already beginning to burst, and if we have to toil overland from here, we may not reach the Klondike before the rest of this tumbling humanity. Reckon there ain't a man among them that isn't capable of jumping our claim.'

They were several hours into the journey before Jim stumbled across his first clue. He'd left Jack to guard their belongings on the main deck, where most of the steerage passengers were situated, while he instituted a more thorough search of the vessel. He was hoping to catch a glimpse of Catherine herself, but a chance encounter brought him face to face with one of her abductors. The gambler had already conducted a fruitless investigation of the two public saloons, and stood waiting to ascend the narrow staircase to the after deck, when a seemingly casual incident triggered his memory.

A well-dressed, and rather corpulent young man with a heavily jowled, florid face, caught in the act of descending the stair, thanked him for standing aside in such guttural and unfamiliar accents that Jim accorded him a second look. Recognition followed at once; he was one of the those who'd followed the unconscious veiled woman on to the *American Fidelity*, a fellow younger than himself, whom the gambler immediately categorized as the son; unable to suppress a grin when he matched the man to Catherine's contemptuous description. He was undeniably fat, and owned a wet mouth.

Following such a large target proved a simple task. Having negotiated a passage for'ard, the fat man laboured up a flight of stairs leading to a wide corridor, where he knocked lightly on a door some half way to its end. As the door opened, Jim pressed past, as though to continue further down the corridor, and risked a quick glance into the room beyond.

It was furnished as a sitting-room, and quite clearly part of a suite, for at least two other doors led off its width. A large picture window provided a view of the sea, and the gambler gained the impression of several others in the room. Walking swiftly, he slid around the next corner and stopped abruptly, swiftly calculating the position of those further cabins. Catherine, he was convinced, must be held prisoner in one.

'Damn.' Returning to the outer deck, Jim swiftly located the position of the two cabins. High up, and out of reach from the deck, lay twin balconies either side of a wide picture window. But even as he swore, a wide grin split the gambler's face. There was still no confirmation of the veiled woman's identity, or even that she was on board, but if she were, it would be an unusual journey for an invalid. He grinned again, entirely sure in his mind that she and Catherine were the same.

'You've found her.' It didn't take much detective work on Jack's part to extrapolate that fact from the happy expression on the face of his partner. 'Where is she?'

'One of the rear staterooms. They've taken an entire suite.' Jim went on to describe the situation to his friend, not even admitting to himself that it may not be the girl's cousin he'd met.

'What now?' Jack looked serious. Kidnapping the girl on a crowded riverboat wouldn't be easy, especially if she were still drugged and unable to back up their story. And nor would keeping her hidden if they were successful.

'I'll have to confirm she's there,' affirmed the gambler. 'It's an easy climb, but exposed.' He stared into the blue above. 'Cloudless, and there's a moon tonight.'

'Wait 'til they disembark,' advised his friend, knowing full well that such cautious counsel would be ignored. Hell, he'd ignore the advice himself, if it were his girl under lock and key.

'I have to know,' Jim confirmed. His heart felt lighter than it had for many a week. It was his turn to play the predator now, no hiding or chasing shadows; he held all the aces.

He took the risk in the early hours. The moon was beginning to wane, though its cool light still lit up the vessel, hiding the first, burgeoning rays of the eastern sun, heralding the new morning.

The climb was simple, and swinging lithely from hold to hold, Jim soon landed on the first of the balconies. A brief search through the open shutters showed a male face, bearded and leonine, occupying one of the beds. Uncle Boris, he assumed. The body occupying the other berth was facing away from him, but its bulk proclaimed the son he'd already met. Jim moved on, taking care to avoid the picture window between the two balconies, completely sure in his own mind that guards would be posted there.

Catherine's face was the first he saw from the second balcony. She lay supine on the bed, but her eyes were open and fixed firmly on his. A brief movement of one white, gowned arm stilled his advance, and a moment later she shot across to the far side of the room to check the door.

'Ho.' Jim spun around, his gaze darting to the seaman below. He wondered how much of his antics the man had seen, but Catherine was equal to the situation.

The gambler barely heard the scrape of the lock behind him, but a moment later her perfume was all around him. She waved at the gaping on-looker, and raising a finger to her lips in the universal plea for silence, flung a silent prayer at his head. 'Please,' she whispered tremulously. 'Don't betray us.' Her other hand had already taken Jim's arm, and a moment later she drew him into the cabin.

'Quiet.' Catherine's mouth lay close to his ear, breathing the words in a soft undertone that left him shivering. 'We're safe enough here, but my duenna sleeps on a chaise drawn across the door.' She secured the opening to the balcony again, and held up the key. 'They don't realize I have this yet.'

Jim swallowed in silent admiration when the soft,

flowing nightdress swirled around her form, clinging lovingly to the curves beneath. She blushed beneath his gaze, and stepped closer, coiling her arms around his wide shoulders, justifying the close embrace by reminding herself that her guard mustn't be allowed to hear their voices. Leaning into him, her face raised tremulously.

'You have a plan?'

The gambler hesitated. A dozen schemes had run through his mind, only to be discarded immediately, but he didn't want to disappoint her. If only she weren't so close he'd be able to think, but his hands were already spanning her slim waist, pressing her even closer. Her face lifted and he kissed her.

'Catherine.' The voice was female and sounded through the door. The duenna had awoken, he assumed; probably the same nurse who'd accompanied her at San Francisco. 'Are you all right?'

'Yes.' Catherine's eyes opened wide in fright, but she retained enough sense to press Jim against the wall where he'd stay hidden by the opening door. 'Come in.'

He loosened the gun in its holster, but stilled at a gesture from the girl. To his surprise, she swiftly loosened the ties to her nightdress and allowed it to drop off her shoulders, holding it protectively across her bosom. The door opened, but before the nurse could enter, Catherine gave her peremptory instructions.

'Please fetch me some water to wash in, Natalia. I find myself unable to sleep, and wish to dress.'

'At this time, my lady?' The attendant's voice remained respectful, despite her dual role as guard.

'It's light enough,' Catherine returned airily.

'Yes, ma'am. I'd better close the shutters if you're to wash.'

'No need. I can deal with that.' Catherine's voice carried a haughty edge of command, and the servant retired, closing the door behind her.

'Hide.' The girl ran across to the balcony, intending to close the wooden shutters, but the deep rumble of a male voice sounded loud outside, and a moment later the door was flung open again.

Catherine had but a moment to release her nightdress, allowing it to drop so far as her waist, while she hid her breasts behind firmly crossed forearms. She uttered an alarmed and alarming shriek.

'How dare you, sir!' The outraged cry disconcerted the new interloper, who closed the door immediately, still mumbling his apologies. The son, decided Jim; Uncle Boris would present a very different proposition.

'Quickly.' Catherine hurriedly gathered up the bodice of her nightdress, a move which, however swift, afforded him a brief glimpse of her bare breasts; pert, uptilted orbs, topped with a splash of the purest pink, pale and beautiful as the sea-coral. Her eyes sparkled mischievously, boldly meeting his startled gaze, before fixing on a walk-in cupboard that occupied one corner of the room. A brief sign, a loping stride, and he stood hidden within, his view of the room limited by the half-closed opening.

The silence was disturbed once more when a large fist beat on the door, followed by a stentorian boom.

'Cover yourself woman.' The voice was used to command, and the man waited only a moment before entering.

'Uncle.' Catherine's voice sounded surprised, then angry when a second person attempted to enter. 'Stay, sir.'

Her uncle ignored the girl, and strode across the room to check the opening to the balcony was secure. The movement brought him directly into Jim's sight. He was an impressive man even in the dubious dress of a nightshirt; at once tall, and broad, and the gambler gained an impression that he would be dangerous when crossed. His neatly bearded face carried an air of nobility, at odds with that of his son's weak-chinned deference, but his eyes glared with the gleam of avarice.

'You'll go back to your bed at once, madam,' he commanded.

'I wish to rise, sir.' Catherine stared back at him fearlessly.

Boris smiled shortly and made a tiny bow. 'As you will, then,' he agreed. He raised his voice. 'Natalia. Come sit with your mistress while she dresses.' A smile crossed his lips while he waited for the servant to re-enter.

'You're very like your mother,' he decided, in a voice that mixed triumph with a measure of respect. 'But Natalia is mine, and whatever plans you may have hatched for escape will be scotched with her at your side.' He laughed shortly, and left the room.

'What do you wish to wear, ma'am?' Natalia's deferential voice spoke from the door.

'I can dress myself, Natalia.' The girl dismissed her duenna contemptuously, and throwing the wardrobe doors wide open, pretended to survey the assembled gowns.

'Yes, ma'am.' Natalia was still out of Jim's sight, but he heard the creak of a chair when she sat down with a resigned sigh. 'I have your water ready.'

'Must you stay?' The girl sounded petulant, but the woman bore her rage with impunity.

'Those are my orders, ma'am.'

Catherine began to sort through the cupboard's contents listlessly, still maintaining a desultory conversation with her guard. She stepped into the wardrobe as though to retrieve a particular gown, and winking slowly, stretched forward one slim, ivory-smooth arm to drop the balcony key into Jim's hand.

'White would suit me best, I believe.' The girl selected some garments from the cupboard and threw them carelessly on the bed. She crossed the room, lost again to the gambler's sight, while she splashed some water into the bowl. 'At least do me the favour of ensuring that Nikolai cannot enter, Natalia.'

The woman vouchsafed no answer, but evidently satisfied the girl, for Jim heard the renewed splash and swirl of water while she completed her ablutions.

'My gown please, Natalia.' She began to dress, a task in which she was interrupted by a polite double knock.

'Who is it?' Catherine's voice sounded apprehensive.

'Just I.' Her uncle's voice was magnified by the opening of the door, and he entered the cabin without further ceremony 'Take her out, Natalia.'

'But....' Catherine's weak objections were immediately overruled by her uncle.

'Do as I say. I have business to transact with this officer.' Uncle Boris didn't raise his voice, but an unmistakable note of command had entered its tone. A rustle of silk heralded the women's retreat, and a moment later the wardrobe doors were thrown wide open again. The startled gambler found himself facing a blue-uniformed ship's officer, backed by two of the crew holding rifles.

'My ward's completely infatuated with the fellow,' Boris told the officer, rolling his eyes towards Heaven in a creditable attempt at sincerity. 'She's an heiress, of course, and not for the likes of him. Ah, it's hard to ensure the honour of a young girl in these rough times. Especially one so innocent and trusting as Catherine.'

6

ESCAPE INTO DANGER

'I demand to see your superior.' The gambler vented all his ire in the request, but none of his indignant railings held any noticeable effect on the impassive faces of his escort. He was frog-marched unceremoniously into the depths of the vessel, and thrust head-first into a narrow, stinking hole, close to the bilges.

'The captain's busy.'

A last glimpse of his captor's smirking face warned Jim the officer had been bribed. No doubt the captain would hear of his captive at sometime in the future, but not whilst Catherine remained on board; they couldn't risk him listening to her testimony. The heavy door slammed shut, leaving the gambler alone in the pitch dark.

'Damn you,' he cried, beating his fists against the unyielding wood. Then, realizing the futility of his actions, he stopped abruptly, and felt his way carefully around the tiny, cramped prison, hopefully searching for another exit. But a brief exploration of the heavy timbers was all that was needed to convince him; there was no escape other than through the solid, oak door, and unable to stand erect under the low beams, he curled up on the floor to await his fate.

'Fire! Fire!' Close on twenty-four hours passed before he stirred to the commotion outside, and a moment later his nostrils picked up the acrid fumes. He flew to the door, pummelling on its rough surface with the desperation of burgeoning fear.

'Let me out,' he roared, contemplating the all too real chance he'd be left to fry.

'You in there, lad?' Jack's voice was quiet, but distinct, and the gambler pricked up his ears.

'Jack.' Jim felt hope flare into life when his partner began to strike at the lock with a heavy implement. 'How did you find me?' The door swung open and he staggered into the flickering light of a lantern held high by his friend. Thick billows of choking smoke caught at his throat, biting deep into his lungs.

'It wasn't hard, matey. The whole ship's aflame with rumours of a felon arrested. Seems like you done just about everything, 'cept bugger the captain's dog. Anyhow, when you failed to reappear, I decided you must ha' been caught, and set out to locate you. There's only so many places to imprison a man on a crowded ship, and what with being at sea since I was a lad, I know of them all.' He began to lead Jim down the confines of a dark corridor.

'Fire!' Jim could hear the renewed warning cries from the deck above, but his partner ignored the furore.

'There was an armed guard over you,' he continued calmly, 'so I set fire to some oily rags, and raised the alarm. They're quite safe, only smouldering, but stuffed down the ventilators they make a powerful lot of smoke. I'd have had you out afore now, but early morning is the right time to make such an attempt; light enough to see, but most folks are still too sleepy to discover the trick.'

'What about the guard?'

Jack laughed. 'He ran like a darned jack-rabbit when he heard the alarm. Probably abandoned ship by now.'

The two men emerged into the pale light of dawn, where Jim was able to survey the results of Jack's fire at first hand. Most of the smoke was lying low over the riverboat's stern, billowing wide in the light breeze, and whipping up hysteria amongst the unfortunate deck passengers without doing any obvious damage. Small groups of the crew were gathering together on the after deck, some striding purposefully through the fumes, and it soon became clear that the ship's officers were beginning to take control.

'Better fetch your girl while they're still panicking,' suggested Jack practically. 'It won't be too long before they discover the fire's a ruse, and you'll need to be in position to jump ship afore then.' He grinned widely. 'There's a boat waiting for you, starboard side, and close by the stern, but watch out for them paddles. We're hove to now, but when they start to roll they can suck you in real quick.'

'You're a marvel.' Jim grasped his partner's hand, and wrung it gratefully. 'I'll see you up at the claim.'

'You can count on it, partner.'

Jim quietly melted into the background, pressing through the rapidly thinning plumes of smoke towards Catherine's cabin. He was no longer armed, but it would have taken a brave man to ignore the fury in his pace, and risk stepping in his path.

'Cat.' He beat on the door to her uncle's suite with a furious tirade of blows.

'Oh.' The door was opened by her duenna, who failed to recognize him in her fright.

'Where's Catherine?' Jim grasped her by the throat. The renewed shouting out on deck contained a note of order entirely missing only a few minutes earlier, and, realizing his time was almost up, the gambler was prepared to forego the niceties.

The servant vouchsafed him no direct answer, but when her eyes flickered unsteadily towards one of the inner doors, he flung her roughly to one side, and inspected the opening. It was a flimsy affair that swiftly caved in under the assault of his boots. Catherine, still in her night clothes, sat primly, perched on the edge of the bed.

'Behind the door,' she warned him calmly, and he slammed it back on its hinges.

Nikolai's shot, spoiled by the surprise tactic, crashed into the ceiling, and a moment later the gambler flung back the ruined door and slammed his fist into the Russian's soft midriff, doubling him over.

'Where's your uncle?' Jim picked up the discarded pistol warily. Intuition told him that the elder man was the more dangerous, doubly so with his all-pervading influence.

'Out on deck.' Catherine was dragging piles of clothing from the wardrobe, 'but he won't stay away for long. This is the first time he's left my presence since you were caught, and only to discover if we'll be forced to abandon ship because of the fire.'

'There's no fire,' Jim assured her.

'Then he'll be back any moment.' She stared long and hard at the gambler. 'He's clever enough to guess it was you,' she decided. 'Perhaps I'd better stay.'

'Not likely, our escape is all arranged.'

Catherine nodded and, grasping a handful of clothing, pulled a warm coat over her nightdress.

They found the boat with no difficulty; a small skiff, containing a pack of basic provisions and a pair of oars. Jim didn't pause to consider where Jack might have found it, or how he'd lowered it into the water without notice; the sailor was a resourceful man who'd had the shelter of night on his side. The huge stern paddle lay still and, as soon as he'd handed Catherine aboard, he thrust away from the lazily drifting steamer and paddled carefully through the muffling smoke, pulling hard for the north shore under its protective cover.

'Do you think anyone witnessed our escape?' Catherine held her silence until they'd left the riverboat far in their wake.

'No one that matters,' Jim decided, doggedly wielding the oars, and grunting under the effort of battling against the current. 'The crew must realize they've been tricked by now, but calming the passengers and getting underway will be foremost in their minds.' He looked deadly serious. 'Your uncle's a different matter; he'll already be out searching for you, if I don't miss my guess. It can't be long before he realizes we must have jumped ship, but even his influence won't have the riverboat turned around once it's underway.'

The boat's keel scraped roughly in the shingle close to the bank, and he jumped out to draw it ashore, where Catherine leapt out nimbly.

'Get dressed,' he ordered, and dragging the skiff into the cover of some bushes, settled down to study the steamboat's progress. Thick plumes of smoke still hung in a miasma over the river, but the air over the ship was already beginning to clear.

'They've located the smouldering rags.' Jim flung the news over his shoulder to keep Catherine informed. 'She'll be moving off soon.' The big paddle began to turn even as he spoke, thrusting the steamer into the current, and on to its destination. A few minutes later, the river rang silent and empty.

'Thank God.' Catherine joined Jim's quiet figure

by the river's edge, her arm hooking familiarly around his waist. She stared at the endless vista of trees around them and shuddered. 'What now?'

'We walk.' Jim shrugged his shoulders, silently inspecting her apparel. 'The ship's due to call at a trading post upstream; can't be too far. I've still got a small store of money, enough to buy some suitable clothes.' He watched her doubtfully. 'Reckon you can walk that far?'

Catherine flushed and bent forward, grasping the trailing hem of her wide skirts. A moment of strain flashed across her face before the material tore, whereupon she unravelled a wide circle, finishing up with a ragged hem line that skirted her ankles. 'The boots might look uncomfortable,' she confirmed, 'but they're sturdy enough.'

Jim nodded; they'd last a day or two. He hoisted the pack up to his back. 'Come on, then.'

The trading-post carried a derelict look about it, an old log cabin, presumably the post itself, and a low built barn behind, overshadowed by the thick growing pines.

'Steamer's come and gone,' surmised Jim, carefully inspecting a rickety pier and the desolate, empty reaches of the river beyond. 'Reckon the owner has too. Wiped out, or gone to join the gold rush more likely.' He stepped forward, Catherine hard on his heels, and stalked across to the entrance. The door swung loose on its hinges, behind it a wide, bare counter. He stepped in, and the blow took him on the rear of his skull, felling him immediately.

He didn't hear Catherine's scream, or see the expression of satisfaction on her uncle's face, nor even feel the blows of cudgel and boot that thudded into his body, not until the onset of night when he awoke, sore and weak.

Even through the mists of pain that swirled over his dulled senses, threatening to pitch him back into insensibility, he knew someone else was in the room with him. Clawing at the last shreds of his waning strength, he attempted to sit up, but subsided again immediately, weak as a new-born kitten.

'You've taken a beating.'

The simple statement was modulated in an educated voice, but Jim recognized the indefinable taint of the killer in it. And I should know, he reminded himself; I've killed enough. Still unable to rise, he rolled weakly to face his captor, a tall, gaunt figure, standing by the blazing fire and thoughtfully hefting a pistol.

'Can you use this?'

The gambler nodded, recognizing the gun he'd confiscated from Catherine's cousin less than a day since. Or was it more? He considered the setting sun, and groaned afresh. He must have been unconscious for several hours.

'Was it you who hit me?' His voice was weak and he felt the red-rimmed clouds of insensibility roll in again.

'No. You were lying on the floor when I arrived.' The words held a ring of truth despite the other's cold indifference to his suffering; likely he'd been abandoned and left to die. He felt the warmth of the fire and realized he might just have done just that without the other's intervention.

'Anyone else around?'

'Not that I saw.' The other pointed towards the doorway. 'The steamer's visited here recently.'

'Yeah.' Jim's head hurt too much for him to puzzle out the other's motive in helping him. He shut his eyes and lay back, trying to assess the extent of his injuries.

'Nathan C. Trimmer. I'm recruiting.' The other had hunkered down by Jim's side.

'Recruiting?'

'I need a fast gun, but anyone prepared to shoot will do at a pinch. Came down here to see old Tom's son; he's a rare one with a pistol, but it looks as though I left it too late.'

Jim surmised that old Tom would be the trader. If so, Nathan Trimmer had indeed left it too late.

'They coming back?'

Jim stared at his inquisitor, wondering how he was supposed to know old Tom's plans. Then realization hit. Nathan Trimmer was nervous of Jim's attackers returning.

'No,' he said shortly, and stirred himself. The world tumbled around him when he made it to his feet, but he leaned on the counter until the dizziness passed.

'They didn't rob you.' The other held out a small roll of bills.

'You're pretty free with your hands.' Jim felt a slow uncoiling of dislike for the man.

Nathan Trimmer shrugged with a cold unconcern. 'Thought you were dead, or dying at least. Probably would have without the fire.'

'Thanks.' That much was true, as Jim well knew, and he fought hard to overcome his distrust of the man.

'None due. I intended to stay here overnight any-how.' Trimmer tossed Jim's pistol across. 'Foreign job.'

'Russian, I expect.' Jim automatically flicked the mechanism to check it was loaded, and thrust it care-lessly into his belt. He wondered whether he'd still be alive if Trimmer hadn't intended to stay at the shack, or even further, if he wasn't searching for men to hire. For sure, his was a cold heart. Abandoning the injured gambler to his fate would have come easy to a man of his ilk.

'You OK?' Inexplicably Trimmer seemed to be interested in his condition.

'Nothing broken.' Jim explored the tender flesh around his rib-cage, and discovered that to be true. There was more pain under his kidneys, but no sign of blood in his spittle, and his head, though it ached abominably, was beginning to clear. He fixed his eyes on his benefactor.

'You say you've got a job going?'

'Long as you can shoot, and don't mind heading for the gold-fields. We'll likely be among the first to make it up there when the snow clears.' He laughed harshly. 'Long as we can avoid the outlaws. They'll be wanting their cut too.' He paused. 'But it's a mighty fine job we got ourselves lined up; enough profit to make us all rich.'

'Prospecting?'

'Not likely. There's more hard work involved in that activity than I ever cared for; easiest way to get rich is to separate a fool from his gold dust.' Nathan Trimmer spat on the floor and stared hard at the gambler, who, fast recovering his strength, was beginning to stretch his limbs. 'You're pretty tough,' he decided. 'If you can travel tomorrow, I may be able to fix you up.'

'Spit it out, mister. What is this job?'

Trimmer watched Jim through narrowed eyes. 'I work for Mr Ryker.' He began as though Jim should have heard the name, but quickly recognized the blank expression on the gambler's face. 'He's about got the entertainment business sewn up at the river-head, and now he wants a slice of the action in Dawson. There's more than enough for everyone from what I've heard, but just to be sure, he sent me out to recruit more insurance.'

'Gunmen!' Jim nodded sagely. So Ryker intended to muscle in on someone else's territory.

'Sure. I've already got a crew waiting for me, but another couple of hard cases will make all the difference.'

'I've already bought into a claim,' declared Jim. He waited to see how desperate the other was.

'That won't matter.' Nathan Trimmer grinned.

'You'll soon change your mind about digging for gold when you realize how easy it is to pick it up in a saloon.'

Jim knew he didn't have much of a choice. If Jack had left the river head before he reached it, Trimmer would be his only method of making the long journey to the gold-fields. He didn't have enough cash left to buy that amount of stores. What he did when they reached Dawson was up to him. After all, he'd already warned the other of his claim.

'Count me in,' he decided.

'Long as you can shoot.'

Jim withdrew the pistol from his belt in a slow, deliberate move, and aimed carefully at the stub of a candle on the mantle above the fire. The slug cut it neatly in two.

7

AN UNLIKELY ALLY

Jim Delaney slept fitfully overnight, only half aware of Trimmer keeping the fire banked high. He awoke with the first faint glimmerings of dawn, feeling drained, but relieved that the pain in his head had settled down to nothing worse than a dull ache. He'd heard of cases where a blow such as he'd suffered could cause lasting damage to the brain, and stood ready to fear the worst.

He rose gingerly, and hobbled stiffly across the room to where his new comrade was brewing coffee, wincing as the tender, bruised flesh tightened painfully around his ribs.

'You ever paddled a canoe?' Nathan Trimmer ignored Jim's disabilities when he put the question.

'No.'

'Didn't expect it,' the man grumbled. 'Just don't slack.'

'I won't hold you up.' Jim spoke the words mildly,

but there was an underlying edge of curtness apparent in his tone.

'That's for sure,' his new companion agreed with bloodcurdling coldness. 'I'll shoot you, if you do.' He picked up his coffee and wandered across to the window. 'We'll leave as soon as the sun hits the water.'

In other words, any time now, mused the gambler. 'You in any hurry?' He'd been hoping for more time to recuperate.

'I've still got a man or two to locate.' Nathan Trimmer began to complain again. 'Everyone who's able bodied seems to have high-tailed it to the workings already, and we're due out ourselves in a fortnight. Tom's boy might have made a difference; he knows the river better'n anyone. Still, he ain't here, and at least you can shoot some.' He made no attempt to disguise his suspicion that Jim would prove a poor substitute for the storeman's son.

The gambler drank his coffee and drew himself together. He made a quick calculation. Jack would have left for the gold-fields by the time they reached the river head, and so would Cat, if it took them anywhere near a fortnight. Uncle Boris would be anxious to claim her inheritance, especially if he suspected that Jim Delaney wasn't yet dead. And neither would Nathan Trimmer consider shooting him; he was capable of it, but he surely wouldn't have come so far to pick up old Tom's son if he wasn't desperate for gunmen to guard his provisions, or whatever it was they were transporting to Dawson.

'Where is your damned canoe?' he growled irritably, aware of an overwhelming urge to consign Trimmer to Hell. But he knew he couldn't, not when the man was offering him a free trip up to the gold workings.

'Hidden,' grunted the killer. 'I realized Tom was long gone from the state of the old place; then again, the door was open. Could ha' been Indians.'

'Hostile?' Jim peered into the trees as though he might surprise a brave creeping up on them. He was thinking of Catherine's party, but Trimmer wasn't to know that.

'Some,' admitted that worthy. 'Ain't had a problem with them myself, but I heard tell of deeds that'd make your hair stand on end.'

'Better get moving then.'

'You ain't told me about the party that attacked you.' Nathan Trimmer stood his ground when Jim limped towards the door.

'I didn't see them.'

'More than one, you reckon?'

'Two at least,' admitted Jim. 'Woman with them too.' He stared at the killer, Trimmer knew more than he was letting on.

'Watched them from across the water,' he explained. 'Four men, two of them sailors, and a woman, looked like she was tied up. The *Queen* was lying around the next turn in the river. Guess they were heading that way.'

So Cat would definitely beat him to the riverhead, mused Jim. Damn her uncle, he must have spun some line to the captain. He'd have bet anything against the river steamer being delayed on account of one woman.

'Why'd they attack you?'

'They were after the woman.' Jim rubbed the back of his head tenderly. 'Guess I'm lucky they didn't kill me.'

'You're in Canadian territory,' reminded Trimmer. 'The law's not always obvious, but even way out here murder doesn't pass without question. Nobody wants the Mounted Police on their trail, especially when they must have expected you to die anyhow. If you should meet them again, remember that. Way out on the Klondike it could be a different matter. Them parts are under American jurisdiction, and Washington's a long way off. The law will arrive eventually, but it's not made it yet. People have been known to disappear out in the wilderness, even in Dawson itself.'

The river was a hard task-master, but Jim's bruised muscles, tempered in the coal-hole of the *American Fidelity* proved well up to coping with the task, and he was congratulating himself on making a full recovery when they finally made the riverhead some ten days later. Not that the gambler was displeased with their progress; the journey would've taken him longer on foot. And besides easing his worries about any lasting injury, the delay had seen him recover the strength necessary to make another attempt to reclaim Catherine from her captors.

Nathan Trimmer wasn't anyway near so pleased.

His recruitment drive had succeeded in netting just one further conscript, a surly and uncommunicative half-breed, whose only qualification for the job seemed to be an unremitting air of brutality.

'He's just the man,' Trimmer had confided in Jim at the time. 'Too stupid to sell us out, and can't wait to fight.' He'd winked knowingly. ''Long as he does-n't murder us in our sleep.'

'Is this it?' Jim turned towards his new boss, appalled by the desolation. So far as he could see the riverhead, from being the town he expected, consist-ed of a string of wood-built stores fronting the river, backed by a motley sprinkling of log cabins, with the last snows of winter still banked up around their walls.

'Yes,' replied Trimmer shortly. 'It doesn't look much now, I grant you, but it'll grow big this sum-mer; the gold rush is only just beginning. The big investors will be moving in soon, and they'll make the real money. Most of the old prospectors are just that. They have no idea of how to develop their finds.'

'I'm looking for someone.' Jim ignored the infor-mation. His eyes searched the snow-shrouded hills beyond, while he wondered if they could have left town yet.

'Too late,' advised his new boss airily. 'This was tent city a couple of weeks back. Now there's nary a soul. Reckon the passes are open already, the weath-er's been so unseasonably mild. Not that the snows are finished yet. There's many an unwary prospector who'll rue the day he set out.' He sniffed the sky as though to verify his gloomy prediction, then stared at Jim's bleak expression and continued, 'There's only one hotel of any note. If you're looking for the woman, you can make your enquiries there.'

'How's this affect your plans?'

Nathan Trimmer shrugged carelessly. 'We leave to schedule if the other men haven't already deserted.'

Jim nodded. If Catherine were gone, he didn't want to hang around either. 'Think they might have done that?'

'I doubt it. Mr Ryker ain't a man to be bilked, and the chance to share in the loot without any hard work of their own should serve to hold them.'

The other hands turned out to be as mean a bunch of renegades as Jim had ever seen; half-a-dozen lean, unshaven desperadoes, whose guns hung low at their hips in well-oiled holsters. The surly half-breed made a good match for them, but the gambler's neat appearance provoked at least one into questioning his role.

'Who the hell's this, Trimmer?' The gang's leader, distinguished by the presence of a bright yellow bandanna about his throat, thrust forward his chin aggressively, but Jim's pistol was already out. He leered in a fair parody of the other's wolfish expression, and ground out his threat.

'No one asks questions, mister. Not about me.' The gun's barrel extended, aimed squarely at the leader's midriff.

The other nodded quietly. 'Guess he'll do.' And

turned away, but Jim had seen the quick flash of hatred in his eyes.

We'll tangle later, he decided, but probably not until we've made the run to Dawson.

'Come on, I'll introduce you to Ryker, Jim. Seems to me you're gonna be a good man to have around in a fight, and he'll want to meet you personally.' Trimmer's tone almost bordered on the friendly in his relief that his hired hands were still in situ.

'Ryker?' Jim wasn't sure that he wanted to meet the man. Neither did he want to meet anyone else. Locating either Catherine or Jack was his first priority.

'Mr Ryker's the boss,' warned Trimmer, 'and not a man to get on the wrong side of. He's greased lightning with a gun, and owns a temper to match.'

'Why me?'

'You're not like the others, Jim. They're gunmen, pure and simple. Killers the lot of them, and as soon kill me as anyone. Ryker's money buys their guns, but that's all they've got to offer. I'll need a deputy to run things in Dawson, someone with a bit of brain, but tough enough to keep the men in line. I saw how you handled Barney back there, it's a job you could do.'

'And why should I meet him?'

'I told you he's got this town sewn up. That includes the hotel.' Trimmer watched the gambler carefully. 'He knows everything that goes on here too. Makes sure he does; if the woman was brought here, he'll know about it. And he'll know where she is now.'

Jim pricked up his ears at mention of the hotel.

Any hotel would act as a magnet to the Russian diplomat, and where he was, Catherine would surely be also.

'That's the place.'

Jim stared at the sprawling wooden shack in astonishment. The building looked sound enough, but even he could appreciate what little planning had occurred in throwing it together. All in all, it didn't look like any hotel he'd ever seen before.

'It doesn't look much from the outside,' agreed Trimmer, 'but it's real decorative when you go in.' He narrowed his eyes at the hubbub surrounding the place. 'Something's going on too.'

A small knot of women, backed by a sprinkling of men were shouting the odds with a pack of mean-looking gunmen by the door, but even as they watched, the party broke up, its end hastened by a warning shot fired over the heads of the crowd from an upper floor window.

'What's up?' Jim tipped his hat politely to one of the women, a strong featured, stern-faced lady of elderly appearance.

'They've got some poor girl held prisoner in there; new in town, and a pretty little thing, too. A bond-woman, they say. She's being put up as a reward for the winner of a prize fight.'

Jim's face paled. 'Thank you, ma'am.' The words were mechanical, uttered involuntarily before he turned back towards the hotel building. Some sixth sense told him the bond-woman and Catherine must be the same. Why, or how, he didn't care. Perhaps

the Russians had finally tired of her rejecting
Nikolai's suit.

Nathan Trimmer's presence saw him past the
guards and into the hotel without trouble, but once
there, the floor was so crowded with men, he could-
n't make any more of the puzzle. Impatiently, he
allowed the trail boss to lead him across the floor and
up a wide, ornate staircase which led to the sweeping
balcony that encircled three parts of the huge room
below.

He paused at the head of the stairs, his eyes taking
in the gaudy grandeur of the interior. The room
below must have extended through most of the
building, with a bar-top that swept completely down
one side, all polished mahogany and brass inlay. The
scarlet hangings, some of them past their best,
looked velvet to him, their brilliant hues highlighting
the huge canvasses, a mixture of gaudy and erotic
scenes set in shimmering gilt frames that hung on
every wall.

Tables and chairs were scattered throughout the
interior, though most of the crowd inside were standing, their faces directed towards the wide expanse of
stage that stood at one end of the room. The curtains
were shut, but Jim had the feeling that something
was expected to happen soon. The next show? He
shrugged uncertainly, realizing he'd hoped for a
glimpse of Catherine's familiar face.

'Mr Ryker. This here's Jim Delaney.' Nathan
Trimmer had left Jim's side to enter one of the doors
that led off the balcony. Evidently it was his boss's

office, for he emerged with the man a moment later.

'I understand you're willing to join my little enter-
prise in Dawson, Mr Delaney.' Mr Ryker's smooth
voice interrupted the gambler's thoughts, and Jim
turned to regard his new employer.

Ryker was a big man, but running to fat from too
much good living. The suit he wore was of expensive
cut, and he should have appeared a great man in the
making, but something was missing to the gambler's
shrewd eyes. He schooled his expression to reveal
nothing of his thoughts, but he'd seen too many men
of Ryker's cut to be impressed. A thief and a bully, he
considered; a man who considered himself too big
for the law. Well, that might be true until the law
reached out across this frozen waste when, like all his
ilk, he'd go too far, and someone would cut him
down. Jim's smile twisted uneasily on his lips. Hell,
that's what he'd done for a living himself one time.

'I'll help guard your belongings, Mr Ryker, but
I've a partner on his way to the gold-fields already. I
can't promise to stay in your employ once I'm in the
Klondike.'

'Fair enough, Mr Delaney.' Ryker smiled expan-
sively. 'But Trimmer reckons you're a good man. I
can't employ too many of those, whatever it costs.
Maybe you'll change your mind once you've travelled
to Dawson with the boys.'

The last few words were spoken in a harsher tone,
and Jim realized that Nathan Trimmer was being
instructed to put the pressure on him to stay.

'Maybe I will,' Jim agreed, without showing any

noticeable enthusiasm. 'What's happening below?'

'I'm sponsoring a prize fight,' explained Ryker. 'The Frenchman there' – his pale hand extended to point out a giant French-Canadian dressed in a suit of greasy pelts who'd climbed on to the stage – 'once fought as a professional. Successfully too, or so he says, until some scandal forced him west.' Ryker smiled, a daunting sight. 'Killed his man, I believe.'

'I heard something about that outside.' Jim kept his voice under tight control. 'You've set a woman up as prize.'

'A bond-maid,' confirmed Ryker. His eyes grew hard, flint-like under lowered brows. 'Some damned foreigner sold her to me as a whore, but she's a lady for all that, and not to be forced. Not like the other one; a quick taste of the switch soon changed her mind.'

'Is it legal to hold her for a prize?' The other must be Natalia, her nurse, Jim pondered. His eyes narrowed, and a powder-flash of fury lit up their depths; had Catherine suffered under the lash as well? For one brief moment Ryker's gaze dropped before the gambler's challenge.

'What else am I to do with her?' Ryker summoned the effort to regain his manner of suave confidence. 'She won't whore, despite all I was told, and no other work would provide a sufficient return on my investment. I considered selling her on, but most of these damned drifters have little enough money, and the real prospectors won't buy.'

'I'd take her as a whore.' Trimmer's eager eyes had

seized on the girl, abruptly displayed when the curtains opened to a fanfare from a single cornet. He
leaned forward, too intent on ogling Catherine's
charms to notice Jim's impatient growl of anger.

'So would a dozen others, Nathan, but there's
enough fools live here to invoke the law, and shut me
down. No, while there're women ready and willing to
whore, there's no need to risk forcing another for
the sake of a quick profit. Properly handled, selling
tickets for the fight will ensure a return on my investment.'

Jim was only half listening to their conversation.
With the advantage of height afforded by his view-
point, he could clearly see the low set dais on which
a young woman was displayed. The dress she wore
was a tawdry impression of *haute couture*, designed to
reveal her figure, and Jim ground his teeth helplessly when a man reached out from the floor to squeeze
her calf through its folds.

Ryker was aware that he didn't have Jim's attention, and quickly remarked on it. 'Yes,' he concluded. 'She's beautiful, don't you think?' He laughed
harshly. 'Jean-Luc does, in any case. He expects to
win her.' He laughed again. 'And I've no doubt he
will.' He paused to rap out a command to those
crowding around the frightened figure of the girl,
who nevertheless managed to hold her head up
proudly. 'Give her space, and stop touching unless
you intend to fight for her.'

The mob drew back, their eyes on the powerful
giant leering at the lovely captive. None of them

intended to fight, not against Jean-Luc, even for so glittering a prize.

'I'll take your challenge, Mr Ryker.' Jim Delaney's glance lay on the giant French-Canadian, summing up his abilities.

Ryker stared at the gambler. 'Jean-Luc is a killer,' he warned him. 'From what Trimmer says, you'd be more useful to me alive.'

'Like I've already said, Mr Ryker, I've a claim awaiting me once your goods are up in the gold-fields.'

Ryker shrugged. 'Then it's your own funeral.' He turned and roared out details of the match to the accompaniment of loud cheers from the floor.

'Take the girl,' he told Trimmer, 'and guard her well.' His glance rested significantly on Jim's tall frame. 'Don't let anyone speak to her until after the fight.' He grinned at the gambler. 'That way, your prize will taste all the sweeter.'

8

LOCATING THE PRIZE

'Was that wise, son?'

It wasn't until later the same evening that Jim Delaney heard the inevitable question couched in a familiar voice. He spun around from his place of honour at the head of the bar, where everyone wanted to buy him a drink.

'Jack,' he cried blissfully, flinging his arms around his partner and twirling him high in the air. 'How long have you been in town?'

'Since the *Queen* docked last week,' the old sailor explained dutifully, 'but we can't speak in here.' He cast a meaningful glance along the length of the bar, where Ryker and his sidekick, Nathan Trimmer, were watching their reunion with a higher degree of interest than it appeared to warrant. 'I've got a powerful lot to tell you.'

The gambler nodded. 'We'll take a walk,' he

offered. 'I expected you to skedaddle off to the gold-fields to establish our claim as soon as you arrived.'

'That was the plan, but I got wind of your girl's problems, and decided to wait on you,' returned Jack. 'Once they had her back on the *Queen*, I figured you wouldn't be far behind.'

'How did it happen?'

Jim was enquiring about Catherine's sudden trans-formation into a bond-woman, not her kidnapping in the forest, as Jack well knew.

'Your foreign friends had need of money. The story's all around town they borrowed against their estates being slap bang in the middle of the gold-fields. Catherine's uncle ought to have known better. Anyone with a lick of sense must have realized they'd be down by the west coast, closer to Mother Russia. There's barely a chance that any of their settlers trav-elled so far east as Klondike territory.'

'Are you saying those lands are worthless?'

'As good as. Won't fetch a brass nickel in this town, any rate.'

'And Catherine would?'

'That's right enough.' Jack looked serious. 'A new girl way out here's worth her weight in gold, particu-larly one as pretty as her, and I reckon Ryker paid through the nose for her services. They say he was real mad when she refused to whore, but there's still some decent folk in town and he didn't dare take a chance on forcing her, especially when the Canadian authorities are already itching to close him down. Pitching her as prize in a fight may show a return on his capital, particularly since he controls the gambling.'

'He said as much,' admitted Jim, then changed the subject. 'What's the word on Jean-Luc?'

'Not good, lad. He's the sort of brute that lives to fight. Makes a living as bully for one of Ryker's competition, so your boss'll be egging you on at least, but the word is that Jean-Luc was in the prize- game until he killed an opponent in the ring.'

'He's out of condition,' hazarded the gambler hopefully.

'Over-age too,' agreed his partner, 'but from what I've heard, I wouldn't lay out money on you beating him. That's one mean bear of a man, and he's set his heart on winning the girl. '

'Trimmer's got her stashed away somewhere.' Jim peered at the old sailor desperately. 'We've got to get her out of town before the contest begins.'

'I'll see what I can do,' agreed Jack. 'There's some folks in town as might be willing to help, so long as they don't have to go up against Ryker's gunmen.'

'Leave them to me,' nodded the gambler. 'You just find out where he's got her hidden.'

The pre-fight hullabaloo figured large in Ryker's plans to milk the fight for every last ounce of profit, a scheme in which both Jim and his rival, Jean-Luc, were expected to play their part. Two large canvas domes were erected, one for each of the opponents, and a sizeable entry fee was charged for the public to watch their preparations.

Nor did the hotel's owner stint on Jim's own training. Despite his oft-spoken reservations on Jim's ability to defeat the big French-Canadian, Ryker knew the general public would see the gambler as an extension of his own image, and somehow managed to turn up an experienced trainer; drink-sodden but still knowing.

'You've a chance, my boy,' that very man told Jim after going to spy on Jean-Luc's training schedule, 'but only a slim one. You're younger and faster; if you can keep out of his way and hold on to your nerve, you might pop one under his guard when he tires.' The trainer sighed apprehensively. 'He's a tough one though, and well used to fighting in a ring. If you allow him to herd you into a corner, you're a dead man. There's nobody out there who's going to pull him off you, that's for sure.'

Small wonder then, that Jim was beginning to feel desperate as the date he was due to fight grew closer. Despite his best efforts, aided by the more respectable elements in town, Jack had to admit his lack of success in locating Catherine's prison on the eve of the big day.

'Damn it, Jack. The fight's tomorrow evening. We've got to find her,' Jim told his friend, holding his voice down to a low whisper. It was evident that Trimmer, at least, had identified Catherine as the girl he sought, and if he knew, then so did Ryker. At any rate, one of that individual's gunmen followed him wherever he went. Discreetly, and at a distance, it was true, but nevertheless galling to the gambler, who couldn't risk making a move to search for the girl himself.

'For your own protection,' Ryker informed him suavely, pretending that his deadly rival, who employed Jean-Luc, would stop at nothing to ensure the French-Canadian won. He smiled wolfishly. 'And further insurance for all the money I've laid out on you and the girl,' he admitted in a moment of rare honesty.

That evening the role of protector had fallen on Barney, leader of the desperadoes so soon to head out for Dawson, and a man with whom Jim had already quarrelled. The gambler eyed his shadow morosely after Jack left, promising to redouble his efforts, and simultaneously caught a brief glimpse of Nathan Trimmer slipping surreptitiously out of a side door. A small gunnysack lay clasped against the folds of his voluminous greatcoat.

A lead! The thought clamoured loudly in Jim's brain; where else, other than to see the girl, would Trimmer be going after dark with a bag of provisions? He slumped back on the bar, still keeping half an eye on his own guard. A fanfare of sounds and the curtains on stage drew back on the night's entertainment, heralded by a tableau of scantily clad women. Barney's attention was distracted a moment and by the time his mind returned to contemplation of his duties, Jim had disappeared.

The dark Arctic night proved at once a blessing and a curse to the gambler. Barney, following through the hotel doorway only a few, scant yards behind him, was unable to spot him in the deep shadows and took off on a wild goose chase, disappearing around the end of the sprawling edifice. Likewise, Jim found himself unable to discern Nathan Trimmer's direction, and it was only the chance opening of a door far up the frozen, mud-streaked snow in the street that saw him on his way. The brief flare of light momentarily illuminated a rapidly flitting shadow, a movement that might not have belonged to his quarry, as Jim well knew, though he guessed that there would be few enough pedestrians abroad at night.

It's got to be Trimmer, he decided. At this hour, anyone else would be heading towards a source of entertainment, not outward bound for the wilderness. A swift, calculating inspection of the hotel environs convinced him that Barney was nowhere in sight, and he set off up the ill-defined street at a loping run.

Once outside the town's boundaries, he found the trail easier to follow. The ground rose in a smooth arc towards the ridge that overlooked the riverhead and from his position lower on its slopes, he caught infrequent glimpses of his target silhouetted against the lighter background of the sky. Across the ridge lay the unending forest, but Jim felt no fear that Nathan Trimmer would escape him; their destination must lie close, close enough at least to allow walking through the drifting snow on a dark, windy night.

It was his voice that gave Trimmer away. The gambler had padded silently into the trees, determined to search every twig if need be, when he heard his quarry order the standing guard back to town. Evidently he was his replacement. Within a minute, a darker bulk erupted from the dark night, passing Jim's silent, hidden figure by only a yard or two, and was gone, showing him the direction he required. An instant later Jim stood outside a small log-built cabin, listening under a leather-shrouded embrasure beside the thick, wooden door.

'Eat up,' he heard Trimmer instruct another occupant. Catherine, he had no doubt, and was rewarded with the evidence to support his conjecture when she spoke a moment later.

'Why? Are you afraid I'll appear too frail for the winner of your contest?' The ill-concealed lash of contempt in her voice lent fresh hope to the gambler. At least her spirit hadn't been broken by the harsh treatment she'd received.

'You don't suppose Ryker intends to waste you on some brute who wins a brawl, do you?' Trimmer laughed, an evil sound that sent tremors shivering down Jim's spine.

'Then what?' Of a sudden Catherine's voice had gathered hope, an emotion that was quickly squashed by the bully inside.

'You're bound for the gold-fields, my girl. The authorities that might seek to protect your innocence here are entirely missing in the hinterland. Ryker intends to desert his properties in town and make a fresh start up the Yukon, somewhere beyond

Dawson, where there are plenty of mining communities growing up without the benefit of law. You'll just be one of the girls up there, so you'd better get used to the idea.'

'What are you doing?' Catherine's voice had changed, rising, with a clear note of alarm in it, and Jim's ears pricked harder.

'I intend to school you myself,' her captor answered triumphantly, his voice almost erasing the small shriek of fear she uttered.

'That wouldn't be wise.'

Nathan Trimmer snarled out his rage when the door opened and Jim ground out his warning. He was caught at a clear disadvantage, his belt already half unbuckled, but despite the odds, he didn't hesitate to fumble for his gun. Maybe he'd seen his fate written in the stony glint in Jim's eyes, but at any rate he died with a gun in his hand; the gambler's unerring aim bringing him down with a single shot.

'Jim.' Catherine jerked at the iron cuffs that attached her to a makeshift bed, flinging herself into his arms when he drew close. It was only the shouting outside, and the sound of distant running footsteps that disturbed their reunion, and she ordered him gone. 'You can't hold them off for ever,' she begged, 'and if you die, then so should I.'

He knew she was right, but not until he realized that her fate was inextricably linked with his own did he move. He knew her location, and could return with the tools to cut her free.

* * *

'I think we need to talk, friend.' The gun jabbed awkwardly into Barney's spine, jerking him upright from his position leaning against the hotel timbers, where several of its clientele still stood watching to see if they could discover a reason for the shooting.

'Delaney.' The desperado breathed a sigh of fear.

'That's correct,' Jim began to explain. 'I don't think Mr Ryker would like to discover that I've been out on my own, do you?' The other didn't answer immediately, and the gambler viciously flicked the barrel of his pistol in a painful swipe to his kidneys.

'No.' The word tumbled out in a painful undertone, while the desperado's eyes began to roll.

'I've been for a walk along the riverbank,' continued Jim imperturbably. 'Just to stretch my legs. The snow's not too deep that way.' He paused significantly. 'I saw you follow.'

'That shot....'

'It couldn't have been anything to do with me,' Jim insisted. 'Not with your eagle eye on me. Shall we go back inside?'

That was all right with Barney, who felt safer without a gun barrel in his back, but he regarded Jim with a glare of pure hatred when he retired to his old position by the bar.

Ryker's anger was a live thing, palpable even in such a large room, and the occupants quickly parted to let him through. Barney was his first port of call, but he soon made his way towards Jim, his gunman trailing dejectedly behind. It didn't take much intelligence to understand the man had spoken as Jim requested; his fear of being found wanting when his boss was so angry had ensured his compliance.

'You been out tonight, Delaney?' Ryker came straight to the point, his face white with strain.

'I took a walk earlier,' admitted the gambler. 'Along by the river.'

'By the river?' The question remained plain in Ryker's voice. He clearly wasn't certain of what he was being told.

'Sure, I needed the exercise. Ask your tool, if you don't believe me. He follows me everywhere.'

'Nathan Trimmer's been shot.'

Jim caught the dawn of sudden understanding on Barney's face, and at another time might have laughed at the flickering emotions warring on the desperado's face. He desperately wanted to betray Jim's secret, but having already lied, he was unable to achieve that without inviting retribution on his own head. Ryker would have been angry to learn he'd lost his charge, but he'd be as stone-cold dead as Delaney if his boss found out he'd sought to deceive him over a matter as weighty as this.

'Can't say as I'm surprised, Mr Ryker.' Jim kept a cool head on his shoulders. 'Nathan Trimmer's hardly the most popular man in town; seems like he goes out of his way to upset folks sometimes.'

Ryker nodded coldly and turned on Barney. 'Fetch Jean-Luc to me, and that mangy boss of his.' A sudden thought occurred to him. 'And where's that

Russian?'

'Russian?' Jim hadn't considered that Boris and Nikolai might still be in town, lying low, and the word was out before he could think coherently.

'No business of yours,' Ryker recovered his poise with an effort and managed a credible attempt to pull the wool over Jim's eyes. 'Just an old tracker I might have to use to follow Nathan's murderer.'

'You saw her?' On the morning of the fight Jim saw Jack for one last time, and brought him up to date on the night's activities.

'With my own eyes. She's there all right; imprisoned in a remote cabin on the edge of the forest, a mile or two out of town. I made some discreet enquiries of my own this morning, and Ryker holds deeds to some land that way.'

'Does he suspect you?'

'Yes,' admitted the gambler. 'He's doubled the guard over me, or I'd have sneaked out earlier this morning and completed the job myself. But I'm not his only suspect. So far as he knows, I went nowhere near her last night, and I managed to induce Barney to back me up on that point.' He smiled grimly in fond remembrance of the gunman's look of pure horror when he realized the snare he was caught in.

'They may have moved her,' Jack surmised.

'Perhaps,' Jim shrugged, 'but it's unlikely they've done so yet. Apart from the fact he's lost his chief lieutenant, Ryker plans to pack Catherine off to the

Klondike before the victor can claim his winnings. If you can persuade someone to keep watch, so much the better, but I'd stake my life on her remaining in place until they leave. We already know he wants her remote from town, and bearing in mind he's about to desert his operations here, how many out of the way places can he own?'

'What if they bring their escape plans forward?'

'They won't.' Jim felt confident that Ryker's greed would hold sway over any desire to play it safe. 'He aims to collect every last penny he can from the fight before quitting town.'

'What about Ryker's gunmen? They won't be in any mind to give the girl up lightly.'

'I dare say she's protected,' argued the gambler insistently. 'But Ryker has installed me or Jean-Luc as the prime suspect, and once the prize-fight is under way no one will be interested in supporting those guards. Of the men he employs, most will be needed to control the crowds here, which will leave few enough to watch over Catherine anyhow. They'll back down soon enough if sufficient numbers of the townsfolk can be induced to show up.'

'Sounds easy.' Jack allowed his scepticism to show through.

'Easier than fighting Jean-Luc,' returned the gambler, shaking his head ruefully. 'You'll need tools though. She's chained to her bed. And watch out for her Russian relations. I don't know precisely where they are, but it's a silver dollar to a split nickel they're holed up somewhere in town.' He thought a moment. 'And you can bet your last dollar they won't have forgotten she's the key to obtaining those estates in Russia; or the title, for that matter.'

9

PRIZE FIGHT

The big event approached all too slowly for Jim
Delaney's taste, despite his realization of just how
desperate his case would be. He knew himself to be a
fit, strong man, who'd benefited from a modicum of
pugilistic training in his youth, but everything he'd
heard and seen in the last few days only served to
convince him further that Jean-Luc must prove too
tough an opponent for one who'd never fought in
the ring before. And having realised that the big
French-Canadian, a bear of a man, would beat him,
Jim quickly perceived his real task must be to survive
the expected battering long enough to offer Jack a
realistic chance at setting the girl free.

The ring itself, made of canvas padded board, and
erected in the centre of the hotel bar, was far too
small for the gambler's taste, who'd banked on uti-
lizing his superior agility to keep himself out of trou-

ble. But as the hour of reckoning approached, he climbed into its claustrophobic environs wearing a carefree smile, and displaying every outward sign of confidence. His supporters too, cheered him on with a heartening show of zealous enthusiasm, a form of favouritism due more, he suspected, to Jean-Luc's unpopularity amongst the masses, than any confidence they felt in him winning the bout. As Jim well knew, the betting had overwhelmingly favoured his opponent. Nevertheless, the noisily expressed maelstrom of support proved a welcome boost to his flagging confidence, and prompted a growing determination that he should live up to their championship. Jean-Luc, himself, was the last to enter the ring, where he commenced to glare at his smaller opponent with every indication of real hatred.

This was the first Jim had seen of the French-Canadian close up since the challenge had been issued. He stood over six foot himself, but his giant opponent dwarfed him, though this was more due to his burly torso than any superiority in height. Neither could all his bulk be attributed to a sedentary lifestyle, the gambler decided. Jean-Luc may have been carrying more weight than in his fighting days, but even from the opposite corner of the ring, he could sense that his opponent was in fine fettle.

'Watch his right,' Jim's trainer advised quietly, still busily lacing up the lightweight gloves they were to fight with. 'He'll try to set you up for a sucker punch to end the bout early. And remember that Jean-Luc's a fighter from way back; he'll move much faster than you'd expect from such a big man, most especially his hands.'

'How long do I have?' This was the first time Jim had voiced his concerns to his trainer, and that individual considered him carefully before answering.

'First round, he'll rush you from the bell, seeking an easy victory, and when that fails you'll have a round or two where he'll spar with you, probing for your weaknesses. If you get the opportunity, try to nail him then. Who knows, after that? Probably a war of attrition, where he'll seek to wear you down gradual like. For sure, the longer the fight lasts, the less your chances of winning.'

Jim smiled wearily. Even if he found the chance to nail the big French-Canadian, those first few rounds would be too early for Jack's benefit. Now he knew Ryker didn't intend the victor to claim the girl, no good could come of winning the bout quickly, if at all. He would have to extend the fight, playing for time, and in using those tactics, play directly into his opponent's hands.

The announcement of the fight was being bellowed over a voice trumpet as they spoke, and Jim stood briefly to wave to his supporters when he was introduced. The crowd roared their encouragement as the appointed referee called them forward, but no polite touching of gloves took place, Jean-Luc was already signalling his ill-humour with a stream of malignant threats.

'I tear you apart, pretty boy. Slowly I beat you, and with much pain.' The big man turned to the crowd and shook one enormous fist at those still daring to abuse him from the safety of the masses. His voice rose in a roar of defiance. 'The girl is mine,' he cried. 'I no forget you.' He pointed directly at a face in the crowd, and then another. 'Or you.'

A bell rang somewhere by the ringside and the French-Canadian surged forward on the instant. Forgetful of his promise to inflict a slow and painful defeat on the gambler, Jean-Luc's huge fists weaved and punched with a speed and accuracy that almost cost Jim the fight there and then.

A flurry of jolting left-handers combined with a right hook to slam through his guard, and leave him wobbling, but though his head was spinning, he used his trainer's fresh advice to good advantage. Covering up, he desperately sought to deflect his opponent's blows, riding a storm that surely couldn't last. Sure enough, the maelstrom of leather began to subside, and dancing lightly on his toes, Jim began to conduct an adroit defence that saw him slip away unharmed by Jean-Luc's more brutal rushes. Most of the blows that slipped past his guard, he rode, his confidence gradually returning, though his head still rang from the effect of that first deadly assault.

The fight had been measured on the basis of two-minute rounds, and Jim was thankful to hear the end of the first round heralded, despite his knowledge that the fight was scheduled to continue until one or other of the men could no longer rise. The timing had been woefully long by his reckoning, but his trainer reassured him while he towelled him down in the corner.

'No, two minutes it was. There's no need to worry, you've got his measure now. He'll have to slow down if he's to last; he's far too heavy to sustain that sort of pace.'

The trainer's experienced advice proved accurate once more, and Jim found a very different Jean-Luc opposed to him at the beginning of the second round. In the giant's eye lurked a measure of regard for his agile rival, a respect swiftly compounded when the gambler began to launch his own attacks, jerking back the French-Canadian's head with a series of well-weighted combinations. Not that the younger man could ever feel the fight running his way, for the other soon showed he had a measure of science as well as sheer brawn to display to the enthusiastic crowd.

The next couple of rounds followed the same sort of pattern. Jim Delaney ducked and weaved, moving with a confident agility to keep his bigger opponent at bay, and launching sudden, swift attacks of his own that staggered the ex-professional without ever pushing him into real trouble. But despite these occasional successes, the gambler could feel the big French-Canadian growing in confidence with every passing minute.

The fifth proved almost disastrous for him. Jean-Luc, confident he had his opponent's measure, began to open up again, catching him by surprise. A beautifully executed dummy set up the gambler to take one of the professional's thunderous right handers, and a torrent of blows crashed in behind to leave Jim swaying under the deluge of punishment. The round was virtually over, and almost out on his feet, he somehow managed to hang on until the end, desperately slipping and dodging by pure instinct alone.

'Take the fight to him,' urged his adviser between rounds. 'He'll come out so confident, you might catch him on the hop.'

Good advice, decided the gambler, and came out of his corner like a raging whirlwind when the bell rang. Jean-Luc, however, failed to display the over-confidence predicted, and rode Jim's desperate attack, picking off his most powerful punches with a display of assured defence that gave a clue to the pugilistic skill that lay beneath his brutal lunges. The smaller man was in no mood to draw back though, and for a moment the two stood head to head slugging it out to a torrent of applause from their supporters.

The seventh gave Jim his best moments. Jean-Luc launched an abortive attack that left him off balance and vulnerable to the gambler's riposte. A straight left, perfectly placed, set up the giant French-Canadian for a potent right hook that left him sagging against the ropes. Jim knew they were some twenty minutes into the fight, and praying that Jack had taken his chance to free the girl, flung himself at his opponent, storming forward with flying fists. His stunned opponent, driven back by the flurry of blows, still managed to keep his guard, but for once it was he rather than the gambler who greeted the bell announcing the end of the round with palpable relief.

The effort entailed in sustaining that attack had, however, borrowed much from Jim's reserves, and the fight began to slip inexorably from his grasp. The French-Canadian made no spectacular gains, but round by round gradually began to dominate his smaller opponent. A mixture of stolid indifference to pain, unremitting brutality and a measure of skill the gambler could never hope to emulate, combined with Jean-Luc's long ago learned ringcraft to take its toll of an opponent whose own agility was being worn down through sheer exhaustion. But again and again, as the next round was announced, he hauled himself off his stool to face his malevolent rival.

'The girl's gone.' The news spread around the ring-side like wildfire, vociferously propagated by the noisy and excited spectators.

'What?' Jim, perilously close to collapse, could only goggle at the crowds swirling around the perimeter of the ring. He stared blearily towards Jean-Luc, a man as surprised as himself, and staggered back to his corner, somehow under the impression that yet another round was over.

'Jim.' The impression that someone was calling him slowly sank through the gambler's consciousness. 'Come on, lad, rouse yourself. We've got to get out of here.'

'The fight,' Jim's voice slurred wearily when he

finally stirred himself to peer at his partner, staring at his face through wary, pain-racked eyes. 'I've got to keep fighting until Catherine's free.' He dropped his voice to a whisper. 'Ryker's got her, you know.'

'That's what I've been trying to tell you. Catherine's escaped.' Jack, reminded of the saloon owner's presence, glanced uneasily towards Ryker, who stood at one end of the room surrounded by a group of his men. 'We've got to leave now, Jim,' he continued in a more determined voice. 'Ryker's already suspicious of you.' He grasped the gambler's arm and began to pull him bodily from the ring.

'Delaney!' Ryker bellowed out the gambler's name and attempted to intercept the escaping pair, but in that was frustrated by Jean-Luc, who apparently held his own suspicions as to who had removed the girl from her imprisonment. The big fighter thrust through the crowds, and barred his way.

'Keep it up, lad.' Jack, forced to switch his attention towards Jim's erratic movements, missed any further developments, worried that his partner might not make it out of the hotel, let alone as far as the hiding place he'd arranged.

'I'm all right.'

A blatant lie. Jim's face ran red with blood, staining his broad chest, and dripping unheeding to the snowy wastes outside the saloon. He began to tip forward, barely conscious.

'Damn it, Jim. Keep a grip.' Jack gave up, and hauling his partner on to his shoulders, began to stagger up the street.

* * *

Jim felt the warmth permeate slowly through his bones, the fresh stirred blood acting to aggravate the pain in his battered flesh. He tried to rise, but weak as a new-born kitten, fell back helplessly, groaning under the renewed ache in his temples. His head swam, and his senses swirled helplessly, his eyes unable to focus properly on the unfamiliar surroundings.

He was lying on a bed, he decided groggily, a very soft bed covered in warm blankets, though the icy cold still ate into his bones. The room was small, with shutters drawn across its windows; was it still dark? He shivered and attempted to push himself up again, but the weight of his coverings defeated him. He sank back, listening idly to a conversation from an adjoining room. Catherine, he decided, though he couldn't make out what she was saying. Was her voice slurred, or his hearing? Was it her cabin they were occupying?

The thought stuck hard. It might be her bed, now being spoiled by his bloodstained carcass. His hand moved warily, pushing at the covers. He was naked, his skin clean. And his face? He felt the bumps and cuts, greasy with the ointments spread to heal. The thought moved on, he'd been washed and doctored, then put to bed. Not Ryker's work, for sure; perhaps they'd evaded him.

Jack's remonstration cut in on his mind's clumsy wanderings. 'Damn it, Catherine, I did it to save his hide.' The old seadog's voice rang loud in exasperation.

'Dragged your partner through the snow, with him barely dressed. He might have froze to death.'

'He'd have died for sure at Ryker's hands,' came the agitated answer. 'That bastard from hell realized Jim was behind your disappearance.' The gambler almost raised a grin; Jack's habitually polite demeanour had been shattered far enough for the old salt to swear in front of a lady.

'You're right.' Catherine's voice was quiet and Jim forced his ears to strain for her answer. 'I'm sorry. We both owe you our freedom, but he's lying there so helpless.' A soft sob rent his heart, a sentiment evidently shared by his partner.

'Don't give up on him, Catherine,' Jack's voice sounded gruff. 'Jim's a tough one. He'll pull through.'

The room fell silent for a few moments.

'You'd better go watch him.' Jack's voice sounded far off, echoing distantly through the gambler's senses. 'I'll get some sleep, and relieve you later.'

The door opened quietly, and was as silently closed again, but Jim decided he was no longer alone. The shadow of a woman spread across his pallet, and he stirred restlessly.

'Jim. You're awake.' A fresh, happy voice slashed through all his wanderings.

'Cat.' The word, simple as it was, came out mangled, but she slipped to her knees by his side, salt tears forming in her eyes again when she scanned his wounds.

'Oh Jim, your poor face.' Her soft fingers feathered across his bruises, as though to soothe them with the power of touch. His hands moved again, and he tried to rise, but fell back once more, shivering in his weakness.

'You're still cold.' Catherine, having made the pronouncement, stood up at once, and began to tug impatiently at the tiny pearl buttons running down the front of her dress.

'Cat.'

Jim watched on helpless while she tore open her bodice, and lithely shrugging her elegant shoulders, peeled the garment to her waist. Another wriggle, and the voluminous skirts were freed, let loose to slip to the floor under their own weight.

'Don't try to speak. Save your strength.' Catherine stepped gracefully out of the tangled garment.

Jim closed his eyes momentarily, then focused on her busily twitching hands. A lacy cloud of petticoats followed the skirt, thrust down to expose her slender legs, and disappeared in a surge of foaming material when she kicked them carelessly aside. She swung around, and for a brief period, all he could spy was her back. Delicately poised, she lifted first one leg, and then the other, to the height of a chair, the better to slip off her stockings, unaware of the soft swell of her bottom flexing gracefully beneath his gaze.

Standing tall again, her shapely legs braced a few feet from his face, she caught the hem of her camisole and stretched high. Mesmerized by her elegant motion, his eyes followed the slow unfurling of the garment, teased slowly off her back, up and over the loose coils of her hair. She turned, and the high-set, pertly uptilted breasts he'd spied so briefly from a wardrobe on the riverboat, swung enticing before his eyes. She bent swiftly from the waist and divested herself of the last of her clothing, a brief, silky pair of bloomers.

'Move over.'

Catherine slid into the bed and adjusted the covers, pressing her body close against his own, both naked as the day they were born. Her arms slipped around his bruised and weary torso, the light touch of her fingers twirling in the thick hair at his nape, gently urging his head to lay confined against her softly welcoming bosom. Slowly he began to relax, abruptly aware of her heat seeping through him, searing his body with its potent life-force.

He draped one leaden arm across her, the tips of his fingers flat against the swell of her hips, beginning to relax. The scent of her perfume filled his mind. His eyes snapped shut, and he slept.

10

A GOLDEN RECOVERY

When Jim Delaney next awoke, he discovered himself alone once more. Shutters still barred the window, but bright shafts of illumination, forced eel-like through chinks in the old wood, displayed the quietly dancing dust in a miasma of sunlight. He raised an exploratory hand to his aching head, tracing the swollen outline of bruised cheeks and lips, while he recollected fragments of the fight. A ragged scar, high above one eye, caught at his fingertips, rough against their calloused pads.

The door opened softly and an anxious face peeped around its bulk. A face on which a smile slowly formed, encouraged by his return to consciousness.

'How are you?' Catherine's quiet voice sent shivers down his spine.

'Bruised,' he returned, 'but not beaten. How do I look?'

'You're not so pretty, but you'll live.'

'Thanks to you.'

'And to that partner of yours.' Catherine blushed scarlet when she realized what he meant; a hot, blood-red curtain that seared across her face and plunged deep beneath the wide scooped neckline of the robe she'd donned.

Jim felt an instant reaction when he recollected her naked body and grinned foolishly. 'I thank my partner, too,' he concluded, willing himself to thrust aside the thought of her bare in his arms. 'Did they beat you?' He changed the subject abruptly.

'You saw my back?' Her eyes collided with his, opening wide on the compassion reflected in their depths, even as she answered her own question. 'Of course you did.'

'I saw.' His voice sounded clipped, curt even. 'And I'll kill Ryker for that one day.'

'No need Jim. He gave up quickly enough when he realized it wouldn't get him anywhere. Didn't want to damage the goods, I suppose.' She dropped her head. 'Natalia fared worse; she never could take pain; Uncle Boris learned that soon enough.'

'You mean....'

'Natalia, not me. My uncle never laid a finger on me. He didn't need to. I'd be married to his son once we were on Russian territory, whatever objections I put forward. Either they'd drug me, or find a priest who wouldn't indulge his scruples too far. Easy enough for a powerful nobleman whose ward spoke no Russian.'

'Cat.' He stretched out a sympathetic arm and tried to rise, but his stiff and battered muscles rebelled alarmingly.

'Jim, don't.' Catherine dropped to his side, cradling his head tenderly against her shoulder.

'It's just a cramp,' he assured her.

'And no wonder,' she declared, a mist of tears threatening her eyes. 'You should never have fought that big ox. Not for me; I'm not worth it.' A tear formed and she dashed the back of her hand across her face, determined not to give in to her weakness. 'I nearly died when Jack showed up with you laid across his back last night. I thought you must be dead.'

'I felt like it,' admitted the gambler. 'Where is the old fraud anyway?'

'Out collecting what news he can, but I expect he'll be back here before dark.'

'Before dark?'

'Yes, it's late afternoon already. You've slept most of the day.'

'How long did you stay last night?'

'Through 'til dawn.' Catherine didn't attempt to misunderstand his question. 'You were cold, and tired.' She stared at him defiantly. 'And I'd do it again.'

'Tonight?' The simple eroticism of his question uncurled slow coils of passion in her belly, but Catherine had no intention of backing down. She stared him out.

'Regain your strength first, lover,' she advised. A

soft, double knock sounded at an outside door, interrupting their *tête-à-tête* and Catherine took the proffered chance to scuttle away.

'So you're awake, lad?'

Jim nodded slowly, and looked into his partner's
eyes. 'Thanks old man,' he started. 'I don't remember much, but for sure I didn't escape Ryker's
revenge on my own two feet.'

'You weren't in much case to do anything,' admitted Jack. 'Reckon it was only concern for the girl that
kept you going.' He grimaced reminiscently at his
first sight of the blood-soaked gambler still gamely
moving forward against his erstwhile opponent. 'You
were a sight,' he concluded.

'And Jean-Luc?'

'He looks near on as bad as you, but he's on his
feet this morning and madder than hell at Ryker.
Reckons that hellion stole the girl away, just like half
the folk in town.'

'Ryker's still here, then?'

'Holed up in the saloon. He's trying to assert that
all bets are off, and holding on to the stakes until he
can match the two of you again. But with Jean-Luc
claiming the girl and a gang of angry prospectors
demanding their money, he's facing an uphill struggle. Just as well, since he'd likely be out searching for
the two of you if'n he could escape them.'

'What now?'

'Gather your strength, boy. Reckon you're gonna
need it, and maybe earlier than you think. We'll light

out for the gold-fields soon as you're fit enough to ride; Catherine won't be safe until we can spirit her out of Ryker's way. Not to mention Jean-Luc. He won't give up on her in a hurry.'

'How's she taking it?'

'Better than I expected,' Jack replied slowly. He watched his partner carefully. 'How much do you remember?'

'Enough.'

Jack nodded. 'She spent the best part of twelve hours in bed with you. Keeping you warm, or so she claimed. Refused to leave until you were sleeping naturally, and even then I had to threaten to drag her out by main force.'

'That figures.' Jim tried to haul his weary body into an upright position, persisting until Jack caught his shoulders and laid him back.

'You've got some mending to do before you move from that bed, lad. Rest today, and perhaps you'll be fit enough to get up tomorrow.'

'Maybe you're right.' Jim relaxed his sore muscles and lay back, closing his eyes. His breathing sounded even in the small room, and Jack left in silence.

'That smells good.' Jack and Catherine looked up in surprise when Jim entered the living-room an hour or two later. He walked stiffly, but without any notice-able sign of pain. Curious, his eyes searched through the cabin. Only the two rooms, he categorized. Rough built, and probably well out of town limits. How the devil did Jack manage to carry me this far?

'You should have stayed in bed.' Catherine spoke in a flat, unemotional voice, willing any anxiety for him out of her thoughts, though the flame of battle lay smouldering in her eyes.

Jim held up his hands in mock dismay. 'I'm hungry,' he complained. 'I wasn't allowed to eat for hours before the fight, and right now, I need some sustenance to keep me going. You can't mean to starve me, Cat. That's no way to treat a sick man.'

'You took some soup earlier this morning.' Catherine's statement surprised him, for he had no recollection of that, only of her warm body pressed against his own. 'Eat then.' She laid a plate in front of him and tipped a scalding mess of stew on it. 'And then you go back to bed.'

' Sure thing, Cat. Will you tuck me up?'

The girl watched him tenderly. 'I'll come,' she promised.

'Well, I'll be off to the saloon myself.' Jack broke into their private world with his sudden decision. 'It's time to find the lay of the land down there. Last I heard, Jean-Luc was threatening to search every cabin in town.' He threw on a thick coat, and paused by the door. 'I reckon he would, too.'

'Where's my gun?'

'Damn the gun, Jim. You get back to bed, or I'll use the serving spoon on you.' Catherine raised the ladle in her hand in a threatening gesture to back up her words.

'You'll come too?'

'I said I would,' she grinned, 'but not until you're

safe under the covers.'

'It's a cold night,' he continued hopefully, 'I'll need you to keep me warm.'

'Not tonight, Romeo.'

Her eyes twinkled, but there was a firmness in her voice that brooked no argument. She wouldn't be sleeping in his bed tonight, he decided regretfully. Though his muscles still ached; unlike the previous evening, he had no doubts about his ability to make love to her, nor of his desire to do so.

True to her word, Catherine came to keep him company on the pallet he called a bed, settling close against his shoulder where he sat propped against the bolster that would pillow his sleep.

'It seems a world away since we first met,' she began hesitantly, and subsided into a brief silence while she sifted through her tumbled thoughts. 'Back then, all I wanted to do was use you, taking what help you could give, and skipping out when it suited me.' She smiled dreamily. 'Now I couldn't imagine life without you.'

'Your father's business partner,' Jim guessed. 'There was no such man, was there?'

'Yes there was,' Catherine maintained stubbornly. Then grinned reflectively. 'But not living in San Francisco. My father's business interests, such as they were, lay further east, Charleston mostly.' She glanced at him coyly. 'John Pym called you Diamond Jim. Were diamonds your business?'

'I'm a gambler,' Jim reminded her gently. 'That name stemmed from the gem I wore in my necktie. I won it in my first serious game, and its reputation just sort of grew with my success.' He sighed. His life as a gambler suddenly seemed far away.

'And before that?'

'What makes you think there was a before?'

'You weren't always a gambler,' she declared passionately. 'I've watched you use that gun like you were born to it, and you're far too impatient to have been confined to smoky saloons all your life.'

'Gamblers can generally defend themselves.' A shadow passed across his face. 'They have to do it often enough.'

Catherine's eyebrow raised in question.

'All right,' he conceded. 'I wasn't always a gambler.' He watched her reaction closely. 'I was brought up on a ranch, way out on the western frontier. My brothers still run cattle there, but chasing cows was never enough for me. I was always different, more adventurous. A wanderer; like my pa, they always told me, though I can only summon up a few childhood memories of him. It was rough out there those days, a bit like Alaska here and now, and a fast gun could quickly earn a reputation for killing.'

'A killer? I don't believe you.'

'I was the sheriff,' Jim explained, 'but you were close enough first guess. I cleaned up the town and made a name for myself. Hell, I almost created a legend. Would have too, if I'd thought to have a diamond at my throat those days.'

'How romantic,' Catherine interposed eagerly. 'It must have been exciting bringing law to the frontier.

I read about such men, but never dreamed I'd meet one. Or—' she dropped long lashes over her eyes in confusion, – 'fall in love with one.'

'There's no romance involved in killing, Cat.' Jim's eyes were hard, remote, as though he hadn't taken in her declaration of love. 'Whatever side of the law you shoot from, a man's left dead just the same.'

'But the law must be upheld,' declared the girl, her eyes wide on his tormented expression.

'So it must.' The self-mockery was evident when he went on, 'But I did it all too well, until one day the truth finally hit me.'

'The truth?'

'I enjoyed the killing,' he admitted, and a twisted smile stretched across his face. 'I did it because I liked the feeling of power I gained when my opponent lay dead at my feet. I loved the adoration of the townsfolk, the way they looked up at me when I walked by.' He laughed harshly. 'But it could never have lasted. When the final badman was dead, I'd have been as loathsome to them as the men I'd vanquished. Not that it mattered. Once I realised the truth, I hung up my badge and drifted. Ended up on a boat on the river, in the middle of a high-rolling card game.'

'Where's your diamond gone?'

'I lost it.' His eyes sought hers in the growing darkness. 'It was stolen a few hours before I met you. They called it my lucky charm, but I never got lucky until someone took it off me.'

'I don't know how you can say that,' Catherine choked, instinctively leaning closer to his presence. 'You've been in one scrape or another ever since we met.'

Jim reached out one hand tentatively, and caught the soft curls over her shoulder, sifting them through his fingers in the wonder of exploration. His mouth approached hers with lazy deliberation, mesmerizing her with its slow progress until his hand gently caught the back of her neck, stilling her fears and blocking escape from his tender kiss.

He murmured soft words of love, and drew her close in instinctive response to the slow unfurling of desire triggered when her lips parted under his gentle caress. Her breasts lay heavy against his chest, and his free hand moved to cup one, gently stroking the yielding flesh through her robe, while its crested peak rose hard, taut against his rasping touch.

'Cat.' He sighed her name, soft as the wind in the trees. And blindly allowed the heat of his mouth to seek the soft, scented hollows at her throat and shoulders while she returned his embrace with knowing caresses of her own.

'Damn.' The expletive hissed from his mouth when the sound of a door opening caught them both by surprise.

'We're in here, Jack,' acknowledged Catherine drawing back with the drugged lethargy of a woman in the throes of desire. Her eyes met those of her lover and she giggled at the foiled air of passion measured in their gaze. 'Wait until you've recovered completely,' she promised with a wink. 'I'll still be here.'

'Can you ride?' Jack burst into the room in a tizzy. His glance took in their close proximity, but he didn't stop to comment.

'Now?'

'Tomorrow. No one travels at night out here, not unless they have to. We'll need to leave early though. I've been doing a spot of earwigging and Ryker will be breathing down our necks. Someone must have let our secret slip; he doesn't know exactly where you are yet, but he's dug up enough clues to conduct a successful search.'

'Where did you learn this?'

'Jean-Luc.'

'Why should he tell you anything?'

'He didn't exactly. He beat it out of one of Ryker's lieutenants, and then faced down the man himself. I'd snuck into the saloon by a back way to listen by the office door. Jean-Luc just burst in and confronted Ryker with his evidence.'

'A foolish move in the circumstances,' decided the gambler. His eyes fixed on the old sailor. 'I take it Ryker killed him.'

'Sure did,' agreed Jack. 'Pulled a gun clean as you please, and shot him where he stood. After that, he had to light out quick, with any of his men he could gather. Jean-Luc had spilled the beans in the saloon before challenging him, and those prospectors with bets still on were after blood.'

'How do we go?'

'I've a parcel of dogs kennelled in the barn out back, enough to pull the two sledges I purchased. I hoped we'd have a day or two to arrange travel with a party, but our packs are already loaded, apart from a few utensils Cat brought in to cook with.'

'I'll be ready,' decided the gambler. Now he had Catherine back, whether he travelled alone or with a party hardly mattered to him.

11

TO THE GOLD-FIELDS

'Are you sure you're ready for this, Cat?' Jim's eyes flickered nervously over the impatiently yapping line of dogs attached to his sledge. Catherine lay on the sled immediately in front of him, bundled in furs amongst a jumble of mining and exploration equipment.

'Don't worry, Jim,' she answered optimistically. 'They'll follow Jack's lead.'

'Mush.' The gambler cracked his whip in the air above the team, fervently hoping her speculation would prove correct. Jack had learned his dog-craft from the old settler who'd sold him the teams, but this hurriedly arranged journey was Jim's first encounter with the animals, following a brief half-hour's tuition from his partner on the theory of driving a dog-sled while they hitched the animals up.

To his relief, the dogs flung themselves against the traces with every sign of gusto and sprinted after

131

Jack's own team. With rather more daring, he essayed a minor adjustment to their course, and felt a shudder of elation shiver through his frame when the rig responded to his command. Half running and half riding the runners, he settled confidently in the wake of his partner.

Several days passed without anything extraordinary happening, and Jim began to breathe easy. Out in the wilderness it was unlikely that either Ryker, or Catherine's Uncle Boris would be able to track them, and the two partners, rapidly learning the basics of dog-care, were soon eating into the miles left between them and the gold-fields. Catherine too, took her turn at controlling the dogs, and at night would snuggle close to Jim in the tiny tent they all shared.

The gambler's stiff, tired muscles had long since healed, and, apart from a ragged weal over one eye, no more than a few fading discolorations testified to the effectiveness of Jean-Luc's fists. His own bruised hands, though still swollen, had lost the stiff knuckled clumsiness of the days immediately following the fight, and all in all, he was sufficiently recovered to count himself lucky not to have taken any more serious hurt.

'Over there.' Jack hauled his team to a halt, and waited for Jim to come alongside.

'What is it?' The gambler narrowed his eyes on the scene. Heavy, snow-bearing clouds were scudding low overhead, and in the fading light the darker patches barely showed against the snow.

'It looks like dead bodies,' decided Catherine. Her face, already wan in the eerie light, showed paler when she realized the significance of her words.

'Yeah, that's what I reckoned,' Jack agreed. Though years older than his two companions, his eyes were still sharp as razors. 'Three of them. Dead for sure, and they're lying on top of the snow.'

'Outlaw attack.' Jim's brief interjection echoed all their thoughts. This was no party of unwary travellers caught in a storm, and buried beneath the terrible force of an Alaskan blizzard.

'Ryker's work, I'll be bound,' conjectured Jack uneasily. 'It's no coincidence that there's three of them; we know he's after us.' The old sailor glanced nervously around, his eyes alert for the slightest sign of activity in the snowy wastes. 'I'll go on in and see what I can find.' He cast a wary eye on Catherine. 'Best if you two stayed put, and kept an eye out for visitors.'

'Sure thing.' Jim relinquished command of his team to Catherine and took over Jack's dogs. Taking out two rifles, he tossed one to the girl. 'If you see anyone, shoot to kill,' he told her shortly.

'It's just as I thought,' confirmed Jack when he rejoined them a few minutes later. 'Gunshot wounds, and not one of them with a weapon to hand.' He held out a faded yellow bandanna. 'Recognise this, Jim? It was lying in the snow nearby.'

'Barney's.'

'I thought so. Those poor travellers were mistaken

for our party is my guess. Ryker's a thief and murderer, but not even he'd bother to set up an ambush
out here, not waiting for the chance traveller.' Jack
allowed his eyes to dwell on the hills that formed
their horizon, and shook his head. 'He knows we
have to travel through that pass ahead. Gonna be
hard to avoid him.' He turned questioning eyes on
the gambler. 'Shall we turn back?'

'Too late for that,' Jim replied shortly. 'We've
already been spotted.' He pointed out across the
snow. 'We're being watched from that bank, about a
mile back.'

'How many?' The old sailor stiffened visibly, his
eyes busily questing in the wake of his partner's
extended arm.

'I only caught a glimpse of them,' admitted the
gambler. 'How about it, Cat?'

'At least two,' she replied calmly. 'They remain
under cover for as long as they can, but they're stalk-
ing us.'

'Keep low behind the sleds,' advised Jack. 'We'll
pull them close and set up camp. At least we'll be
able to defend ourselves; on the move, we give them
a sitting target.'

'No.' Jim hunkered down under cover of the
sledges. 'Drive on slow. They're out of effective range
at the moment, but not for long.' He slipped down
until he was hidden in the snow and lay prone, fin-
gering his rifle menacingly. 'This is my job. I'll provide them with a surprise or two, then catch you up.'

'Jim.' Catherine's eyes held on his for long

moments, then dropped. She gave in and took up the traces. 'Be careful,' she advised.

Careful! Jim almost laughed aloud. Ever since he'd teamed up with the girl, he'd been chased and harried. It was his turn now. Calmly he cocked the rifle and snuggled deeper into the snow, shuffling his hips to dig himself a deeper trench as camouflage. A moment later, satisfied of his concealment, he stilled, patiently allowing long minutes to pass while the light faded slowly under the menace of the coming storm. A shadow flitted along the ridge to his right and he fired, rolling free of the snow in the same movement.

One man stood crouched immediately in front of him, his mouth still slack in astonishment at the gambler's sudden appearance. Jim fired again, at point-blank range, and raced for the cover of the ridge, his feet stumbling in the deeper drifts. The second of his stalkers had cried out when he fell, but Jim had no idea of whether the wound was fatal or no. He had no time to find out either, his initial target had disappeared, and there might have been others.

In the lee of the low ridge he stopped to take stock. Thirty yards behind, the man who'd dropped lay still, dead or too badly wounded to worry the gambler, and a low moan from above signalled the position of another wounded man.

'Shut up, Digger. He'll hear you.'

Jim recognized Barney's voice. No more than the three of them, he guessed; Barney wouldn't be so worried at him overhearing if they had numbers on their side. He rose and surged over the brow of the ridge, levering his weapon with the familiarity of the gun-fighter. Barney half rolled, and slumped under the hail of bullets, while his companion's pistol jerked into the air, firing uselessly.

'Where is he? Where's Ryker?' Jim's fist grasped a handful of the wounded man's shirt, jerking him into a sitting position. A rattle sounded deep in the rene-gade's throat and he hung limply in the gambler's grip.

Jim spat out an oath and flung him back to the ground in despair. Slowly and carefully he examined each of the others. All of them lay dead.

Still a killer, he jeered at himself. And all for noth-ing. Ryker was surely waiting ahead.

A rattle of gunshots sounded nearby, and Jim's self-critical mood disappeared on the instant. Reason told him that Jack and Catherine were involved, so he took off in their wake, ploughing through the deeper snows at a wallowing run. The clouds seemed to have banked up around them, and an eerie twi-light bathed the neverending white of the landscape.

'Jack!' Jim dived under cover of one of their sleds, where the stolid figure of his partner was squeezing off shots into the gathering dark. 'Where's Cat?'

'She's out there someplace, Jim. I let her get ahead, thinking to protect her, until we stumbled right into a nest of these vipers.'

Jim peered into the dark. The wind was gathering itself to blow a gale with snow at its heart, and visibil-ity was rapidly diminishing. No one was firing at them any more, but he sensed the gang still remained out there, waiting to nail them once they left the meagre cover afforded by Jack's sledge.

'Delaney.' Ryker's voice roared out the challenge, but the gambler had no intention of betraying his presence.

'I know you're there,' the gang boss continued. 'You and the girl.'

'D'you think she evaded them?' Jack's question was couched in a low whisper, but Jim waved him to silence.

'It could be a trap,' he suggested, then raised his voice. 'What do you want, Ryker?'

'Only the girl. You and the old man can go free.'

Jim thought carefully. He had no doubt that Ryker wanted the girl, or that he and Jack would be shot as soon as they showed themselves. Had Cat managed to evade capture by some miracle? He didn't see what Ryker had to gain by pretending not to hold her prisoner.

'The girl stays.' Jim tried an evasive answer, hoping to discover more from his enemy, but without success. An eerie silence spread over the landscape, broken only by the yapping of their dogs, hungry now they'd stopped. One growled viciously and began to stalk the two men until it tangled in the traces. Jack searched hurriedly through their packs to throw a loose handful of frozen meat in the direction of their animals.

'Those damn dogs will be eating us if they don't get fed properly,' he grumbled. 'They'll soon grow tired of frozen scraps.'

'I trust them further than I do Ryker,' answered Jim frigidly. His eyes bored into the gathering darkness striving to make out any signs of movement. Their enemies were arguing out in the snow.

'We'll all freeze to death without shelter.' Ryker's voice told the gambler nothing he didn't already know. The temperature was dropping rapidly with the onset of the storm, and combined with the peril of snow to come, shelter and warmth would be necessary to sustain life.

'Just us two,' Jim decided finally. 'Man to man. A pistol fight.' He stood up and moved forward cautiously, despite the covering mantle of darkness. Ryker had a reputation to uphold and he didn't expect the man to back down, especially while his gang were so obviously complaining, but one could never tell.

A low murmur of appreciation told him he was right. Ryker would have to fight to maintain his position.

'Over here.' There was a note of resignation in the gang leader's voice, but Jim was taking no chances. He stopped in his tracks and called the man forward.

'Just Ryker,' he warned the others and slid wraith-like into the eye of the storm, leaving the echo of his voice to attract any assassination attempt.

'Where the hell are you?' A deeper shadow loomed out of the murk with an irritated growl.

Jim stepped forward quietly, throwing his rifle carelessly to one side. Ryker's hands were empty, and despite the cold, his coat lay wide open to display his guns. They faced each other, almost within touching distance in the fading light.

'It's your play, Ryker.' Jim thought back over what he'd heard of the man; he'd seen Ryker kill before, and knew his reputation wasn't over-played. His own hands felt clumsy of a sudden, and a thrill of fear rippled down his spine. His fingers were still swollen from the prize fight, no longer stiff, but undeniably less supple than they'd been. Was this where his life would end? Dead at the hands of a faster gun in the icy wastes of a frozen wilderness. He swallowed hard, his eyes fast on his opponent's bleak stare, barely visible in the darkness. None other would see them fight, but one must surely die.

Some second sense warned him of Ryker's impending move and his fingers flashed to close on the cold butt of his pistol. A sudden blur of movement and he was shooting. Two sharp explosions shattered the Arctic silence, and Ryker dropped, while Jim back-pedalled swiftly away from the scene, half expecting the outlaw gang to open up on him.

'Ryker.' One of the gang called out nervously, but there was no answer and silence reigned a little longer.

'Delaney.' One of them could stand it no longer. 'We've no argument with you. Keep the girl for all we care. We're setting up camp.'

Jim stayed silent a moment longer, waiting until a dark form stepped forward, hands held high. He chuckled in relief.

'Do what you want,' he conceded.

*   *   *

The two friends spent a restless day sheltering from the storm in a makeshift tent hurriedly thrown up in the lee of the sled, while the dogs dug into the drifting snow close by. The blizzard, having raged all afternoon, continued throughout the night and well into the next morning, while Jim tortured himself with images of Catherine freezing to death in the drifting snow.

At first they took it in turns to hold guard in case the renegade gang should return to attack them, but Jack soon realized the futility of that precaution.

'This is madness,' he remarked, gesturing at the ferocity of the storm around them. The air lay black as night to give weight to his conviction. 'There's no point in keeping watch while this blizzard endures; no man could live out there without shelter.'

'No,' Jim agreed shortly.

'Catherine will be all right.' Jack spoke awkwardly, instinctively realizing what was eating at his partner. 'She knows as much about survival out here as we do.'

Perhaps more, Jim considered, trying to still his fears. The girl was a fast learner, and this was, after all, their first real experience of an Arctic blizzard.

Early signs that the storm was dying came late into the following morning when the rattle of snowflakes no longer sounded so loud on their makeshift canvas shelter. Everything outside was white, and when they first peered out it seemed impossible to tell what was sky and what was ground, until a hump appeared almost under their feet and one of the dogs crawled out.

'Better get those animals fed.' Jim crawled out into the open and stood in the slackening wind. 'I'll go see what Ryker's men are at.'

The gambler moved off into the last flurries of snow, mentally assessing the direction of their temporary encampment. A low hump in the drifting snow guided him to their erstwhile enemies, who were also beginning to stir.

'What you want, Delaney?' His questioner's voice was guarded, but contained no hint of real malice.

'This all of you?'

'No.' The man searched around with puzzled face. The snow had ceased to fall and only a few flakes still whirled on the slackening wind. 'Those damned Russians are missing,' he concluded, 'but I expect they'll be around here someplace.' A look of comprehension dawned. 'Come to think about it, I ain't seen them since the storm began.'

The picture fell into place for the gambler. Catherine had been captured before they'd come under fire from the outlaws. Not by Ryker, but her own kinfolk. He laughed harshly, a mirthless cackle that left the outlaw bewildered; there'd been no point to the fight, not for any of them.

Recalling his position, he considered the landscape carefully. They couldn't have got far before the storm struck in its full fury, but would undoubtedly be travelling again soon, if not already. There was no sign of a dog sled, but visibility was still minimal, and the Russians, used to living in such a climate, may have read the weather well enough to have left earlier.

'Set the dogs to,' he yelled to Jack, and began frantically to unhook the load from their sled.

'What in tarnation?' His partner began to question the orders, but Jim interrupted him before he'd finished.

'They've got Catherine. Boris and that son of his.'

'How?'

'Luck, I guess. She must have run right into them. Anyhow, they've vanished, and it doesn't take a genius to realize they wouldn't risk running while this blizzard still raged, unless they had a very good reason. Catherine is the only answer I can think of.'

'You're right, lad.' Jack backed up the gambler's play. 'What about tracks?'

'In this?' Jim indicated the fresh snow. Sharp gusts of wind still tore into its surface to swirl it into tiny whirlwinds effectively covering all but the most recent signs of activity. 'They'll head west,' he concluded confidently. 'Probably got no more than a few miles start on us, and with a lighter load, we're bound to catch them.'

'Keep the supplies,' begged Jack. He too, began to throw out the heavier items of equipment. 'We can always come back for the rest.'

12

FINAL RECKONING

Jim's stony face reflected his unrelenting enmity towards Catherine's abductors, a hard, callous expression that boded ill for the Russian transgressors should he ever catch up with them. The pair travelled throughout the day, heading due west towards the distant peaks, and even when dusk began to fall, the gambler insisted they must keep on the move until the light was completely gone.

'We've no time to waste,' he asserted in glacial tones. 'Once they reach those mountains, we'll never track them down.'

They spent an uncomfortable night under a makeshift canvas shelter, dozing fitfully, with Jim anxious to hitch up the team as soon as dawn's first herald sprang across the eastern sky. As they moved off, Jack expressed his unease over their route. Though the air had long since calmed, they still hadn't cut across the track of another sled.

'Are you sure this is the way, lad?'

'Damn it, Jack. It has to be west. Where else would they head for?' The gambler's harsh façade crumbled, and all of a sudden he looked years older. If the Russians weren't heading toward the Bering Straits and the sanctuary of Mother Russia, they could be anywhere, and for certain he'd lose Catherine. Abruptly he realized how much that mattered to him.

'I guess you're right.' Jack read his partner's face, and made an attempt to mask his uncertainty. Travelling west was chancy, but Jim's was the risk, and he alone owned the credentials to take that gamble.

A scant few hours later his persistence paid off.

The nature of the terrain, if not its perils, had subtly changed as they moved further west into the Alaskan hinterlands. They were now riding across a harder ice, with higher, more mountainous territory slicing their route ahead. Yet another storm was brewing on those inaccessible peaks, and every passing minute found the darkening clouds settle lower across their path as visibility began to drop again in the wake of the scudding squalls.

'There they go!'

Jim was riding the animals hard, determined to use what light there was while it lasted, but it was his keen-eyed partner who first spied the tracks left by their fleeing enemies. The shallow impression left by the dogs and twin runners of a sledge ran almost parallel to their own course, and the gambler immediately swung onto their trail.

'They can't be far ahead,' he muttered. 'Those marks are edged too sharp. Hours, maybe even minutes.' He cracked the whip above the dogs' heads, urging them to still greater speed.

'They've swung around.' Jack, still avidly searching the horizon for any sign of their enemies, made the discovery, and pointed away north, his forehead creased in puzzled dismay. Their quarry had inexplicably plotted a new course, one that saw them running at an acute angle to their pursuers, but in the opposite direction.

'Where the hell are they heading now?' The gambler turned their sled to head off the other party, who, he realized, must have lost valuable time in changing direction. In a fearful moment of doubt, he began to question whether they'd cut across an entirely innocent group of travellers, so unlikely was the new course.

Until Jack's sharp eyes picked up the reason.

'Crevasse,' he pointed, gesturing urgently.

Jim narrowed his gaze beyond the fleeing sled and picked out an outline of the yawning gap that had caused the Russians to change their plans. He followed the stark, jagged line with his eyes until he saw what they were heading for. A slim bridge of ice that stretched precariously across the fissure. And beyond that, what appeared to be a solid wall of ice, barring any further progress.

'They'll never make it.' Jack's eyes were fixed on the delicate structure, and he shouted out the warning while Jim calculated a new course, heading directly towards its span. Both of them watched help-lessly as the Russian sled approached the awesome gap and, despite their misgivings, took the icy bridge at a run.

'Go for it, Jim,' Jack screamed when it became obvious the Russians had succeeded in crossing the narrow arch. 'They'll have it down otherwise.'

The Russian sled stopped, almost as though they'd heard his words, and two figures detached them-selves. One immediately began to empty his rifle at the delicate structure, while the other slithered clos-er to take a shot at its profile.

'Damn them.' Jim swore violently when a wide swath of ice detached itself from the bridge with a loud crackling.

'Hold it, Jim.' Jack barked out the order in the wake of this catastrophe. 'It won't take our weight.'

That the bridge wouldn't hold the sled was obvi-ous. Even if their weight didn't bring the precarious structure down, it was no longer wide enough to accommodate the runners. Nevertheless, Jim launched the sled recklessly towards it, only to be balked by the dogs who refused to face its menace, or maybe found themselves frightened by the renewed bursts of gunfire.

Jim realized that Nikolai, Boris's son, was targeting them rather than the bridge, and leapt off the sled, drawing his pistol. Though the range was still long for such a weapon, he fired, and fired again.

Nikolai immediately abandoned his exposed posi-tion by the edge of the crevasse and turned to run towards his father when, with a rumble like distant thunder, the ice cracked and buckled beneath him. With a terrible, despairing shriek, he began to tumble back towards the chasm's wide maw as a broad swath of ice and snow crumbled under his feet, and disintegrated into the crevasse.

Sensing that a wholesale collapse was imminent in the wake of the gunfire, whose echoing crackle still sounded deep in the depths of the fissure, Jim raced to cross the rapidly foundering bridge. Ignoring both the danger to himself and the last, dismal howls of despair from his enemy, who was inexorably sliding towards an icy grave, he leapt on to the icy span. A final, awful shriek marked the conclusion of Nikolai's plummeting fall as the gambler threw himself off the narrow bridge and on to the solid packed ice, scant yards from the Russians' sled.

Boris was already whipping the dogs into a run when Jim's pistol fired again, its brief crack heralding the thunderous crash that marked the final disintegration of the bridge. And Jim's ears had barely recovered from its tumultuous shock waves, when it was followed by yet another almighty roar when the wall of ice before them split, spilling an avalanche of frozen debris across the Russian's path.

For a moment, the air was full of powdered snow, rising around them like steam, while wicked shards of ice sliced across the frozen terrain. Jim, who was still running blindly into the maelstrom, smacked hard into the solid bulk of Catherine's uncle, who'd been thrown off his sledge by the force of the impact.

The two mortal enemies, both stunned into momentary inactivity by the force of the collision, stared at one another while they fought for breath. Boris, desperate, and realizing he must fight for his life, was the first to recover. With a speed that seemed totally at odds with his bulk, he leapt into the attack, sweeping Jim's pistol from one nerveless hand before the gambler could react.

The Russian weighed in as the heavier man, but older and less agile than his opponent, he was more interested in seeking a weapon than in trading punches with a man who'd gone forty rounds with the formidable Jean-Luc. Having divested Jim of his armament, he fell back, intent on gaining the precious seconds necessary to pull out a viciously curved weapon, more machete than knife. A sullen smile spread across his face and he began to stalk forward, confident he held all the aces.

Jim's own knife had mysteriously disappeared, but there was no trace of fear on his face when he faced the bigger man. He'd caught the Russian against all the odds, and he didn't intend to allow Boris to escape at this late stage. Ignoring the wicked slash of the diplomat's weapon, he caught his breath and ploughed forward into the attack, only half aware of Catherine's horrified scream.

The Russian brandished his weapon threateningly, but unable to discover an opportunity for attack that wouldn't lay him open to one of Jim's own swift lunges, backed off. Another lunge, and he riposted wildly, slicing through the gambler's enveloping coat

to the flesh beneath. A blood-red stain spread quickly across the stiff material, as, caught off balance by
the sudden shock, Jim slipped and half fell, provid-
ing the Russian with yet another opening.

Diving forward precipitately, Boris raised his knife
high for the killing stroke, his gaze intent on tracking
the gambler's frantically squirming body across the
ice. Desperately, Jim kicked out at his adversary's
feet, entwining his own legs with those of his opponent and bringing him down with a heavy crash on
the slippery surface. Boris cursed and twisted in the
gambler's grip, attempting a back-handed chop with
his evil weapon that saw Jim forced to scramble for
his life. And before he could recover, the Russian was
upon him again, slashing savagely with a two-handed
grip, yet still foiled in his attempts to land the fatal
blow.

Caught at close quarters, the two began a frantic
hand-to-hand struggle, rolling and clawing at each
other, while Jim fought to keep the lethal weapon at
bay. Close matched as they were in the beginning,
the Russian was by far the elder, and slowly began to
wilt under the strain of his exertions. For a moment
it was touch and go, but gradually the younger man
seized the initiative, and twisting two-handed at the
Russian's wrist, forced him to relinquish his knife.
Boris gave the weapon up with a roar of dismay, but
the fight wasn't quite over yet.

The diplomat was still a dangerous opponent at
such close quarters, and squeezing Jim in a strength
sapping bear-hug, he flung them both towards the

crumbling brink of the crevasse. Realizing the gambler would have no mercy, and that his own defeat was certain, Boris seemed determined to drag the American to Hell with him.

Catherine screamed another warning, but neither man was in any position to attend to her. They rolled closer to the fissure, still crushed face to face, while Jim desperately attempted to land a punch that might stun his opponent.

'Argh.' Boris was the first to realize the full extent of their danger, and releasing his grip on the gambler, he reared back from the very edge of the precipitous fall. Catherine, her arms still bound securely behind her, arrived on the scene in a rush, throwing her full weight against the small of his back, and, with a howl of fear that echoed that of his son so short a period before, the Russian tumbled over the precipice, plunging to a hideous and certain death.

Jim, pale faced from shock, and still clinging tenaciously to the slippery slope above the chasm, threw himself into the helpless girl's path as she too slithered inexorably in the Russian's wake. Hanging wearily on to a jagged knob of ice, he gradually hauled her back to the safety of more solid ice.

13

ALL ALONE

For long moments, Jim and Catherine lay panting on the very edge of the slope that tilted into the crevasse, listening to the last hollow echoes of her uncle's fall.

'Are you two all right over there?' Jack's anxious voice floated across the void, interrupting their silent meditations.

Jim sat up wearily and began to untie the girl's tethered hands. He called back.

'We're alive.'

'Just about,' agreed Catherine quietly, rubbing her welted and bruised wrists to start the circulation going again, while Jim stared at the dark abrasions with anger flaming back into his eyes. 'I thought he was going to kill you.' Her eyes misted over in reaction to the terrible scenes, and she began to shiver in the chill wind.

'Better get under cover.' Jack's words were all but

carried away by the approaching storm, but they brought the gambler back to an awareness that their plight was still desperate.

The avalanche that had blocked the Russian's escape had all but buried the sled and its team of dogs. A few of them, whining piteously, had dug themselves out of the snow in a tangle of traces, but there was nowhere near enough left to pull the heavy sled, even if Jim could free it from its icy grave. Thank God, he acknowledged, that Catherine had been secured at its rear. That part still stuck out of the ice at a crazy angle, one more clue to the weight of ice that held the rig fast in its frozen maw.

'Jack's right,' he told the girl firmly, realizing how close she stood to hysterics. 'Where did they keep their camping gear?'

'In there someplace.' Catherine hauled herself upright and staggered over to the wreck of the Russian sleigh. She shook her head in despair. 'We'll never get it out.'

'Sure we will.'

Picking up Boris's discarded machete, Jim set to work with a will, slicing through the traces of those dogs he could find, before he tore at the huge blocks of ice covering the sled.

'An ice-house.' Jim stared at Catherine's face in the gathering murk. He looked so stunned, she went on to explain. 'My mother often told me how the native Eskimo made houses of ice, and once, in a particularly cold winter, even taught me how to build one.' She dragged out a huge block of ice and pushed it up against the wall of ice that hemmed them in. 'It's easy,' she exclaimed.

The gambler remembered tales he'd heard himself of the strange ice-built houses. Igloos, they called them, though he'd never seriously believed in their efficacy, other than as a barrier against the icy winds. Still there was no other form of shelter available, and the building would, at the very least, occupy Catherine's mind. She hadn't mentioned her uncle's death as yet, but it would be sure to prey on her mind that she'd taken his life. He stepped forward and began to help, supplying her with blocks of ice, hacked into rough rectangular shape by the sharp blade of the machete.

Snow began to fall again, cutting off their view across the crevasse, where Jack himself was preparing to face the perils of the oncoming blizzard, and still they worked on. The resulting structure rose slowly off the ground in an irregular circle of ice that was gradually closed, and under Catherine's instructions, Jim soon found himself placing the final block on its roof.

'What about a door?' he yelled, perplexed by the unyielding surface of the thick, icy walls he'd helped to construct.

'We'll tunnel our way in,' she replied shortly. 'Digging a trench under the walls will help the shelter remain draught proof.' And turning away, she began to salvage what furs she could from the wreck of the sledge, while the gambler hacked gamely at the frozen, hard-packed snow and ice beneath their feet.

The job was a long, hard slog, and by the time he'd completed it, the blizzard was well and truly underway. Catherine had occupied her time by covering the makeshift shelter with loose snow and ice to make a hemispherical hump, and as soon as the trench was deep enough to take her, she squirmed inside, dragging as many furs as she could muster. Jim thrust the remainder after her and slid lithely through the hole himself.

In the dim interior, he could barely discern Catherine's busy figure, though she was rubbed close against him by its small dimensions. He sensed she was spreading the furs under their bodies and roused himself to aid her, extinguishing the last of the light by thrusting a huge, stiff deer hide down the entrance tunnel to block off the gusting wind that flung whorls of soft snow around their temporary home

A strange, harsh scratching sound heralded a flash of light which revealed Catherine kindling a match to light the lantern she'd salvaged from the sled. An eerie, flickering light illuminated the interior, and Catherine took refuge in his arms. Huddled together for warmth, the two took stock of their situation, trapped in an icy cavern of their own making while the thunder of an Arctic storm rumbled overhead.

'Jack will find a way around the crevasse.' Jim spoke with confidence. His partner was a resourceful old bird, and once the storm had done its worst, he'd soon seek out their resting place.

'I know,' Catherine shifted in his embrace and grimaced at him, 'but he'll take a day or two.'

'You saved my life,' he continued, and would have gone on, but she stilled him.

'And you mine. The danger's past now.' She raised her face and planted a kiss on the sharp plane of his jaw. 'It's getting warmer already,' she declared. 'I believe that happens in these shelters. The Eskimo have to strip off their clothes very quickly, else their sweat would freeze when they re-emerge.' She jerked at the fastenings of the thick coat covering her from head to foot, and began to wriggle out of its enveloping folds.

'Strip?' Jim asked hopefully, shucking his own long overcoat.

'Oh yes,' she replied artlessly, busily unfastening her dress. 'I don't suppose we'll need to wear any clothes at all.'